MILE POST 77

MILE POST 77

by

Lorien Kestrel Rye

Third Edition

ISBN: 979-8-90417-513-9

Printed in the United States of America

"All that we see or seem is but a dream within a dream."
— *Edgar Allan Poe*

CONTENTS

CHAPTER 1

1

Evan Mercer hated freeways.

Not in the way most people hated traffic—idling engines, endless brake lights, the creeping frustration of lost time. Evan hated the *speed*. The closeness. The way dozens of vehicles hurtled forward in tight formation, separated by nothing more than painted lines and mutual trust.

He preferred back roads. County highways. Two-lane stretches that curved gently through forests and farmland, where traffic thinned and the air felt less compressed. Roads where mistakes unfolded slower. Where you had time to see danger coming.

That preference had been forged early.

He was fourteen when it happened. A family trip. Clear skies. Light traffic. His mother at the wheel, his father half-asleep in the passenger seat, and Evan in the back, headphones draped around his neck, watching the world blur past.

A truck several cars ahead blew a tire.

The sound came first—a violent *bang*, sharp enough to cut through music and conversation. Shredded rubber exploded across the lanes. His mother never saw the fragments until they were already skidding toward them.

She swerved.

Metal screamed. Glass burst. The world lurched sideways, then spun.

When everything finally stopped moving, the freeway was silent except for distant horns and the ticking of cooling engines.

Both his parents were dead at the scene.

Evan survived, though the doctors used the word *lucky* in careful tones. His right arm had snapped badly, the bone breaking through skin. His left hand was crushed between the door and the collapsing frame. It took multiple surgeries to save it. Months of physical therapy followed, the slow, agonizing process of rebuilding strength and control.

During one of those long, dull recovery weeks, Evan asked his grandparents for a lock.

Just one.

Something he could manipulate. Something that required precision.

They bought him a small practice padlock and a beginner's lockpicking kit. He discovered, almost immediately, that the repetitive motion—the tiny, deliberate movements—gave him focus. Calm. Each soft click of the pins falling into place was a moment of control in a world that had spun violently out of it.

The hobby stuck.

Years later, Evan owned hundreds of locks. Antique padlocks. Modern deadbolts. Combination safes. Practice cores. Puzzle locks.

He carried a slim pick set everywhere, the tools resting in his pocket like a talisman. When he was stressed, tired, or thinking through a problem, his fingers often moved on their own, working through invisible mechanisms.

It was a habit he barely noticed anymore.

Which was why he had chosen Highway 101 instead of the faster inland route.

The Pacific coast stretched out beside him, gray and restless under a low blanket of cloud. He was driving north from Orick, California, making his way home to Philomath, Oregon after finishing a job at the small airport in Willows. Field systems engineering paid well, but the work took him everywhere—isolated airstrips, neglected infrastructure, forgotten facilities quietly failing behind locked doors.

It was midday, though the thick overcast dulled the light, flattening the world into muted shades of green and gray. The forest pressed close to the road, towering redwoods and dense undergrowth swallowing sound and distance alike.

Evan had just passed mile marker fifty when his phone rang.

He glanced at the dashboard display. *John.*

He sighed and tapped the steering wheel once before answering. "What's up?"

"Hey, Evan. You still in California?"

"Just crossed into Del Norte County," Evan said. "Headed home."

There was a pause on the line—brief, but heavy with implication.

"I've got another job for you," John said carefully.

Evan closed his eyes for a moment. "John. I just finished a six-day run. I was told I'd be done."

"I know. I know. And I wouldn't ask if it wasn't important."

Evan exhaled slowly through his nose. "Where?"

"Longview, Washington. Train yard. They're having intermittent failures in one of the switching control systems. They need diagnostics and infrastructure checks."

"That's five more hours north," Evan said. "Minimum."

"I'll give you a full month off after," John said quickly. "Paid. No calls. No emergencies. You disappear."

That gave Evan pause.

A month of quiet. No service tickets. No midnight drive-outs. No emergency reroutes.

"Send me the details," he said at last.

"Already done. And Evan?"

"Yeah?"

"Thanks. Seriously."

The line crackled.

Static surged across the connection, the audio breaking into fragments.

"—signal—losing—"

"John?"

Only static answered.

The call dropped.

Evan stared at his phone, waiting for the bars to reappear.

They didn't.

A moment later, his GPS screen flickered, recalculated, and then went blank.

"No," Evan muttered. He tapped the screen. Nothing happened.

"We live in the twenty-first century," he said aloud, "and there are still dead zones."

He drove another mile before spotting a small gas station tucked into a clearing beside the road. A single pump stood beneath a weathered canopy. A squat building sat behind it, its windows glowing warmly against the gray.

Evan pulled in.

Inside, the station smelled faintly of coffee, oil, and cleaning solution. A young man stood behind the counter, tapping idly at his phone.

"Hey," Evan said. "My GPS went out, and I need directions to the nearest place with lodging. Do you have a map? I've got a long drive ahead of me."

The young man brightened instantly. "Sure do!"

He leaned forward, name tag flashing under the fluorescent lights. *Caleb R.*

The badge sat slightly crooked, pinned to his hoodie at a lopsided angle.

"C'mon," Caleb said, already heading toward a rack of folded maps. "We've got the old-school stuff."

They stood shoulder to shoulder as Caleb flipped through laminated pages, finally pulling one free.

Evan hesitated, looking at the folded the map. "I'll take it."

As he paid, Caleb leaned casually against the counter. "We don't get many visitors out here. Where ya headed?"

"Longview."

Caleb's eyebrows rose. "That's a haul."

"Yeah."

Caleb followed him outside, whistling softly as he circled the sedan. "Nice car!"

"Thanks," Evan said flatly, unfolding the map across the hood. "Where exactly are we right now?"

"Right about…" Caleb leaned in close, pointing. "…here."

"That's… mostly forest," Evan said.

"Yup. Lots of it." Caleb nodded proudly.

"And the nearest town with lodging?"

"That'd be…" Caleb squinted, tracing roads northward. "Klamath." He tapped a small label. "Klamath River RV Park. Or across the river at Klamath's Camper Corral."

"I don't have an RV," Evan said, gesturing toward the car.

"Oh, that's alright," Caleb said cheerfully. "They might just let you sleep in the car. At least until you're rested enough to get to a bigger town."

Evan nodded, committing the layout to memory.

"You're lucky you stopped," Caleb added. "Fog's been rolling in thick lately. Gets weird out there."

"Weird how?"

Caleb shrugged. "Hard to say. Sounds wrong. Lights bend funny. People say the woods move."

Evan glanced at him.

"I mean—probably just stories," Caleb said quickly, laughing. "Locals love their legends. Keeps things interesting, right?"

"Right."

"Sorry," Caleb said, rubbing the back of his neck. "I don't get many new faces. I tend to ramble."

"It's fine," Evan said, folding the map. "Thanks for the help."

"Drive safe!" Caleb called as Evan pulled away.

The fog rolled in less than ten minutes later.

At first it clung low to the forest floor, drifting lazily between the trunks. Then it thickened, rising to swallow the road. The world beyond his headlights dissolved into shifting gray.

The radio crackled with static, fragments of music struggling through interference. Evan tried adjusting the tuner, but nothing cleared the signal. He drove on in silence.

The light faded quickly. Too quickly.

"Shouldn't be this dark," he murmured.

Then the road vanished.

A massive redwood lay sprawled across both lanes, its trunk splitting the pavement like a fallen wall.

Evan slammed the brakes.

The car screeched to a halt inches from the bark.

Heart pounding, he sat frozen for a moment before forcing himself to breathe. He stepped out, inspecting the bumper. No damage.

The fog pressed close, damp and cold.

He scanned the roadside, searching for a way around the tree. The forest loomed dense and impassable.

"Maybe if I had four-wheel drive," he muttered.

Back in the car, he studied the map. Based on his speed and the distance traveled, he pinpointed his approximate location. A quick check out the window to verify his location, he saw what he was looking for.

Mile post 77.

Looking back at the map, he found a thin side road branched off several miles back.

It might bypass this section.

He turned around, found the road and took it.

Four miles later—

BANG.

The car lurched violently to the right.

Then another *bang.*

Evan fought the steering wheel, guiding the sedan onto the shoulder. Gravel crunched beneath the tires as he stopped.

He stepped out, phone flashlight slicing through the fog.

Both right-side tires were shredded.

"What the hell..."

He walked back along the road, scanning for debris, nails, sharp rocks—anything. Nothing lay in sight.

Whatever had done this was gone.

He checked his phone.

No service.

"Great. Now what…" Evan murmured.

The forest pressed inward. The fog swallowed distance. The road behind him vanished almost instantly.

Walking back to the gas station wasn't an option.

Not in this.

Not alone.

He leaned against the car, staring into the shifting gray, and tried to think.

CHAPTER 2

Evan sat in the driver's seat, hands resting loosely on the steering wheel, listening to the quiet tick of the cooling engine.

The fog pressed in against the windows, swallowing everything beyond a few feet. Headlights cut pale tunnels into the haze, revealing nothing but swirling white.

He checked his phone again. No service.

The silence felt heavy now — not peaceful. Expectant.

His mind began running through options. Stay until morning. Let the fog lift. Walk back the way he'd come, slow and careful, until he hit Highway 101 again. South. Civilization. People.

He locked the doors again, though they were already locked.

Time stretched.

At some point he dozed.

Not sleep — not fully. Just drifting, slipping, snapping back awake whenever the car shifted or the fog thickened.

Shadows began to form in the mist.

Tall shapes. Narrow shapes. Things that moved when he wasn't looking directly at them.

Once, he thought he heard his name.

"Evan."

He rolled the window down an inch, heart hammering.

Nothing.

The wind stirred the treetops. Something creaked. Somewhere, far off, something snapped.

He shut the window and leaned back, exhaling slowly.

It was just fatigue. Adrenaline. Fear. His mind filling in blanks.

Still, when a soft tap sounded against his window, he nearly leapt out of his skin.

He jerked upright, fists raised, breath locked in his chest.

Another tap.

"Hey," a man called gently. "You alright in there?"

Evan blinked, focusing.

A truck idled in the road beside him, hazard lights blinking amber through the fog. A tall man stood outside, wearing a dark one-piece work jumpsuit, boots muddy, hair cut high and tight like old military regulation.

His face was lined, but calm.

There was a pale scar along his jaw.

Evan cracked the window.

"Yeah," he said hoarsely. "I think so."

"Mind unlocking the door?"

Evan hesitated only a moment before unlocking the door.

The man stepped back as Evan opened the door, giving him space.

"What happened?" he asked.

"Tires blew. Both on the right side. Hit something I couldn't see."

"Yeah," the man said quietly. "Fog's bad tonight."

They walked back to inspect the damage. The rubber was shredded nearly clean through, hanging in strips from the rims.

The man crouched, running his fingers over the torn edges.

"Road debris," he murmured. "Or something thrown up. Hard to say."

Evan wrapped his arms around himself, suddenly aware of how cold he was.

"I'm Derek," the man said, standing. "I work maintenance at the lodge a few miles up the road."

"The lodge?"

"Old place. Rooms, food, heat. You don't want to be stuck out here overnight. You want a ride?"

Evan hesitated.

Something about the fog, the shadows, the voices — his instincts screamed at him to stay put. To wait. To keep the car between him and the forest.

But the cold was sinking deeper now. His muscles were stiff. His eyelids heavy.

"Okay," he said finally. "Yeah. That sounds… good."

They transferred his bags into the back of Derek's truck. Evan locked the car out of habit, even though he knew it didn't matter.

As they pulled back onto the narrow road, the fog thinned just enough to show towering trunks rising into darkness.

"The lodge been around long?" Evan asked.

"About a hundred years," Derek replied. "Started as a hunting retreat. Expanded over time. Rooms added, wings built. Modernized the utilities, kept the character."

"Sounds… big."

"About a hundred guest rooms. Two stories. Dining hall. Bar. Big common areas. People come out here to disappear for a while."

Evan watched the fog slide past the headlights.

"Disappear," he echoed.

Derek gave a faint, humorless huff. "From the world, I mean."

They rounded a bend, and suddenly warm yellow light bloomed ahead.

The lodge emerged slowly, like a ship rising from fog.

It was enormous.

A sweeping, timber-framed structure with deep porches and massive beams, warm light glowing through dozens of windows. Stone chimneys climbed toward the misted sky, smoke drifting lazily upward. Rocking chairs and swinging benches lined the wraparound porch, their chains creaking softly.

The building radiated warmth.

Safety.

Evan felt his shoulders drop for the first time in hours.

"Wow," he breathed.

Derek parked near the entrance and cut the engine.

"Welcome to the Lodge."

Inside, warmth wrapped around Evan like a blanket.

The lobby opened upward through two stories, thick beams crossing overhead. A massive stone fireplace dominated the far left wall, flames crackling behind a wrought iron grate. Deep couches and overstuffed chairs clustered around it, upholstered in warm earth tones. Bookshelves lined one side, filled with worn spines and small curios.

The scent of wood smoke, baked bread, and something savory filled the air.

It felt... impossibly cozy.

"This place is unreal," Evan murmured.

"We hear that a lot," Derek said.

They crossed toward the reception desk at the back of the lobby. Behind it stood a man in his mid-thirties, soft-spoken and kind-eyed, his posture relaxed.

"Jonah," Derek called. "Found one in the fog."

Jonah's gaze lifted, warm concern immediately filling his face.

"Are you alright?" he asked Evan gently.

"Yeah," Evan said. "Just tired."

"Understandable. Let's get you checked in."

As Jonah typed, Derek gestured around. "Dining room and bar are to your right. Living area to the left."

Evan glanced behind Jonah toward a plain wooden door with a metal sign: **BASEMENT — AUTHORIZED ACCESS ONLY.**

"That's just the basement," Derek said casually. "Boilers, storage, infrastructure."

Jonah handed Evan a keycard. "Room 214. Second floor, east wing."

As if on cue, a young man hovered nearby, holding a tray of empty dishes.

"Miles," Jonah said. "Can you show Mr. Mercer to his room?"

The young man startled slightly, then nodded.

"Yeah — yeah, sure."

They climbed the wide wooden staircase, footsteps muffled by thick runners. Warm light spilled from wall sconces, casting soft shadows.

"My name is Miles. Miles Grant. So," Miles said nervously. "Uh. What do you do?"

"Systems engineering," Evan replied.

"Oh. Like computers?"

"More... industrial. Mechanical systems. Infrastructure."

Miles nodded, processing. "That's cool. I think. I mostly just clean."

They reached Evan's door.

Miles swiped the card, pushed it open.

The room was stunning.

Exposed beams. A king-sized bed piled with thick quilts and soft pillows. A stone fireplace along one wall. A balcony door framed by heavy curtains, faint fog visible beyond.

The bathroom gleamed: stone floors, a massive glass-walled shower, and a deep soaking tub beneath a window.

Evan exhaled slowly.

"This is... incredible."

Miles smiled shyly. "Elena's cooking tonight. You should come down. All meals included."

"I'll be there."

"Bar drinks cost extra though," Miles added.

Evan smiled faintly. "Not much of a drinker."

"Soup's on first," Miles said. "Mrs. Calder insists."

After Miles left, Evan wandered the room slowly, touching the thick wood furniture, the heavy blankets, the smooth stone sink.

He showered, letting the hot water pound tension from his shoulders. The bathroom smelled faintly of cedar and citrus. He shaved, changed, and felt human again.

When he returned downstairs, the dining room glowed with golden light.

A long polished bar stretched along one wall, dark wood gleaming. A handful of guests murmured quietly at scattered tables.

Behind the bar stood a broad-shouldered man in his late fifties, eyes sharp, posture relaxed.

"Evening," the bartender said. "What can I get you?"

"Just a soda, please."

The dining room glowed warmly beneath hanging lanterns and wrought-iron chandeliers, their warm light reflecting softly off polished wood and stone. Round tables filled the space, most of them occupied, though conversation remained subdued, as if the room itself encouraged restraint. A low fire crackled in a massive hearth at the far end, filling the air with the scent of cedar and spice.

The man nodded. "Sam."

"Evan. Thanks Sam." Replied Evan, he paid, tipped Sam and then walked over to an empty table.

"Oh, you must be our traveler," she said warmly. "I'm Rosa. Sit, sit — you look half-starved."

Rosa set a bowl before him first — a velvety squash soup finished with cream and herbs, steam curling upward in fragrant ribbons. Fresh bread followed, still warm, its crust crackling softly as he tore into it.

"You remind me of my nephew," she added, adjusting the napkin at his place. "Always running himself into the ground."

"Feels that way," Evan admitted.

As he lifted his spoon, another woman approached — tall, composed, eyes sharp and assessing.

"Mr. Mercer," she said. "I'm Marlowe Trent. Manager."

Her voice was warm, controlled, confident.

"We're glad you made it here safely."

Evan met her gaze, feeling suddenly seen.

"Thank you," he said. "I don't think I would've managed the night out there."

She smiled faintly. "The forest isn't forgiving."

They spoke of his work, his travel, the isolation of long drives. Marlowe listened intently, remembering details, anticipating his questions before he asked them.

Then came the main course: braised short ribs so tender they barely held together, resting over roasted root vegetables glazed with honey and rosemary. A side of wild rice, studded with mushrooms and dried cranberries, completed the plate.

Evan stared at it for a moment.

"This is… included?" he asked quietly.

Rosa smiled. "Of course, dear. Eat."

He did — slowly at first, then with growing appreciation. Each bite felt indulgent, grounding, comforting in a way he hadn't realized he needed. By the time he finished, the tension he'd carried all day had loosened its grip, replaced with a heavy warmth that settled deep in his bones.

Afterward, instead of heading straight for his room, Evan wandered.

The living room space felt like something lifted from an old-world hunting lodge — soaring ceilings crossed by thick wooden beams, towering stone fireplace, deep leather couches and oversized chairs arranged in loose circles. Bookshelves lined one wall, packed with hardcovers and worn paperbacks alike. Next to them stood an enormous flat-screen television.

He stopped in surprise.

"That work?" he asked.

Miles, who had been stacking firewood near the hearth, nodded. "No cable, though. But we've got movies." He gestured toward a cabinet beside the shelves, filled with DVDs arranged neatly by genre.

Evan browsed until one caught his eye.

"Jurassic Park," he murmured, smiling faintly. "Haven't seen this in years."

"Good choice," Miles said. "One of the favorites."

Evan slid the disc into the player, kept the volume low, and settled into a corner chair near the fire. The familiar opening music filled the room softly, blending with the crackle of burning logs. For a while, he let himself disappear into it — dinosaurs, chaos, nostalgia.

But exhaustion crept up on him faster than expected.

By the time the characters reached the island, his eyelids were heavy. He paused the movie, returned the DVD to its sleeve, and placed it back in its exact spot on the shelf.

Upstairs, the halls were quiet, thick carpets muting his footsteps. As he reached his room, he nearly bumped into Miles coming out, arms full of Evan's used towels.

"Oh — sorry, sir. Fresh towels for the morning are in your bathroom, sir."

"You don't have to call me that," Evan said. "Evan's fine."

Miles flushed faintly. "Right. Sorry. Habit."

Evan unlocked his door. "I might go out walking tomorrow. See if I can find cell service somewhere."

Miles hesitated.

"There isn't any," he said. "Not really. Most of the time I forget I even have a phone."

"That isolated, huh?"

"Pretty much."

Miles shifted his grip on the towels. "Just… keep your patio door locked at night. The woods get…" He trailed off, then gave a small, awkward shrug. "Weird."

Evan raised an eyebrow. "Weird how?"

Miles shook his head quickly. "Just — weird."

Evan smiled faintly. "Noted."

Evan changed into a pair of pajamas and climbed into his huge warm bed and got comfortable under the heavy comforter.

For the first time in days, Evan felt grounded, safe, and he dozed off into a dreamless sleep.

And somewhere, deep beneath the lodge, machinery hummed softly, unnoticed.

<u>CHAPTER 3</u>

He slept deeper than he had in weeks.

When Evan woke, pale gray light filtered through the tall windows, and the distant hush of wind through trees filled the silence. For a few moments, he lay still, disoriented, then slowly remembered where he was.

Breakfast surpassed dinner.

Fresh fruit, thick slices of French toast dusted with powdered sugar, eggs cooked exactly to his preference, bacon crisp but not brittle, and coffee rich enough to feel almost indulgent.

Halfway through, a woman stepped up to his table.

"Hi," she said brightly. "I'm Elena."

Evan swallowed and wiped his mouth. "Evan. And — this is incredible."

She laughed. "You say that now. By day three, you'll be spoiled."

"How did you get into cooking?" he asked.

She leaned against the doorway. "Family thing. My grandmother cooked for half the town. I grew up in her kitchen. Learned early that food makes people feel safe."

He nodded thoughtfully. "You're very good at it."

A faint blush crept up her cheeks. "Careful, or I'll start expecting compliments."

She walked back into the kitchen, still smiling.

Later, Evan stepped onto the wraparound porch.

The fog that had swallowed the forest the night before had retreated, leaving the lodge bathed in pale morning light. The air smelled clean — pine, damp earth, distant salt. Around the immediate grounds, visibility was nearly perfect.

But beyond the perimeter, the fog lingered, thick and unmoving among the distant trees.

Evan wandered the gravel paths, admiring the craftsmanship of the building — the fitted stonework, the carved beams, the careful attention to detail. The lodge felt solid, ancient in the best way, like it had grown naturally out of the forest rather than been imposed upon it.

Warning signs dotted the edges of the trails:

DANGER AT NIGHT

STAY INDOORS AFTER DARK

DO NOT ENTER FOREST AFTER DARK

He paused at one.

A faint sound drifted through the air.

Whirrrrrrrrr.

Soft, but constant.

Evan followed it around the side of the lodge until he found a large electrical meter mounted beside a utility shed. The disk inside spun rapidly, almost blurring.

"That thing's always like that."

Evan turned.

Derek stood a few feet behind him, one hand resting casually on the handles of a wheelbarrow filled with tools — shovel, rake, tarp, a small chainsaw.

"Always?" Evan asked.

"Fence pulls a lot of juice," Derek said. "Whole property's electrified. Keeps animals out."

"Animals?"

Derek smirked faintly. "Predators. Bears… among other things." He added under his breath. "We are in the California redwoods after all."

Evan nodded slowly, eyes drifting back toward the fog-wrapped trees.

"Never know what's out there," Derek added lightly.

"Doesn't look that threatening."

Derek followed his gaze. "Looks can be deceiving."

He started to walk away, then paused.

"Don't get caught out there after dark," he said casually over his shoulder. "The woods get weird."

Evan stood there long after Derek disappeared around the corner, listening to the steady hum of electricity and the distant sigh of wind through unseen branches.

Something about the place felt… off.

Evan lingered outside a while longer, breathing in the clean, salt-tinged air. The quiet pressed in around him, not oppressive, but thick — the kind of silence that made every sound feel louder by contrast. A distant bird call. Wind whispering through unseen branches.

It felt good.

He hadn't taken a real vacation in years. Time away from work usually meant hotel rooms near industrial parks, the smell of oil and concrete, the low hum of machinery leaking through thin walls. This place felt like a world apart — insulated, insulated enough that the rest of life barely seemed to exist.

Eventually, responsibility crept back in.

Evan headed inside, making his way toward the reception desk where Jonah stood quietly sorting paperwork.

"Hey," Evan said. "Any word on when the phones might be back up?"

Jonah offered an apologetic smile. "Not yet, I'm afraid. Derek's working on our end, but the damage up at the highway was extensive."

"I was wondering if maybe he could drive me into town so I could make a call," Evan added. "Just to let my boss know I'm alive."

Jonah's smile tightened, just slightly.

"I do apologize Mr. Mercer," he said carefully. "But Derek isn't permitted to transport guests while he's on duty. Liability reasons. If something were to happen..." He let the sentence trail off.

"Right. Of course."

"Last night was an anomaly, he knew he shouldn't have picked you up, but with the phones down, and well... it being past dark."

"I understand Mr. Pike, it's alright."

"We can arrange a car service once the lines are back up," Jonah continued. "And in the meantime, if it helps, we'll happily comp your stay, Mr. Mercer."

Evan blinked. "That's not necessary."

"Ms. Trent feels awful that you're stranded," Jonah said gently. "Please."

They went back and forth for a moment, Evan insisting it wasn't needed, Jonah calmly refusing to budge. Eventually, Evan gave in, more out of fatigue than agreement.

"Alright," he said. "Thank you."

Jonah inclined his head. "Of course."

Evan wandered toward the dining room, remembering the games he'd glimpsed the night before. The room was quieter now, the breakfast crowd long dispersed. Sunlight filtered through tall windows, casting soft patterns across polished wood.

In the corner, near the hearth, a lone man sat at a chess board.

He leaned forward, elbows on knees, fingers hovering just above the pieces. His brow was furrowed in concentration, lips pursed slightly as if he were arguing silently with himself.

Evan paused, then crossed to the bar.

"Tea, please," he said.

Sam poured it without comment, sliding the mug across the polished surface.

"Sugar? Creme?" Sam asked.

"Sugar, please."

Sam grunted softly. "Of course." And slid a sugar bowl towards Evan.

"How'd you end up working out here?" Evan asked, spooning sugar into his tea and stirring.

Sam glanced toward the windows. "We were here when the place opened."

"We?"

Sam studied him for a moment, "Rosa and I. We've always been here."

"Always?"

Sam's mouth twitched. "Feels that way. We were both here during the fire."

"Fire?"

Sam's gaze drifted, unfocused. "Eighties. Took half the place with it. Thought that was the end."

"And?"

"Marlowe's father bought the land. Rebuilt it from the bones up. Bigger. Better." He paused. "And... Rosa and I stayed."

Something in his tone made Evan wonder what *stayed* really meant.

He took his tea and approached the chess board.

"Mind if I join you?" he asked.

The man looked up, blinking slightly, as if surfacing from deep thought.

"Not at all," he said. "I could use the distraction. I've been arguing with myself for ten minutes."

"Dangerous opponent?"

"Terrifying," the man agreed, smiling faintly. "Ian."

"Evan."

They shook hands. Ian's grip was firm but careful, as though his joints bothered him.

They reset the board and began.

Conversation came easily — the kind that drifted naturally between moves.

Evan talked about his work, troubleshooting failing systems in places most people never thought about. Ian nodded, eyes lighting with recognition.

"Infrastructure analysis," Ian said. "I work adjacent to that. Data logistics, mostly. Pattern recognition. Failure forecasting."

"Then you understand," Evan said.

Ian smiled. "More than I'd like."

They talked shop, overlapping in places, diverging in others. There was comfort in the shared language of systems and logic — a shorthand understanding that required no translation.

After a while, the conversation softened, drifting toward travel, exhaustion, and the strange pull of isolated places.

"I've been so tired since I got here," Ian admitted. "Must be the fog. Or the quiet. Feels like it gets inside your bones."

Evan nodded. "Like the world slows down just enough for you to notice how fast you've been moving."

"Exactly."

The game ended in stalemate.

Ian leaned back, stretching. "Well. I suppose that's fitting."

"Draws always feel more honest," Evan said. "Neither side really wins."

Ian chuckled. "I like that."

He stood, collecting his jacket. "I'm going to take a nap. Might as well enjoy being stranded."

"Fair enough."

They exchanged a brief nod before Ian headed for the stairs.

Evan returned to the living room, selecting a book at random and sinking into a chair near the fireplace. The soft crackle of flames and the distant hush of the forest lulled him into a state somewhere between alertness and sleep.

Miles moved quietly through the room, straightening chairs, returning misplaced books, adjusting pillows.

Evan lowered his book. "Hey."

Miles startled slightly. "Oh — sorry. Didn't mean to disturb."

"You didn't. Have a seat and tell me, how'd you end up working all the way out here?" Evan asked. "Young guy like you."

Miles hesitated, but sat down on the chair next to Evan's.

"My uncle got me the job."

"Lucky."

A faint smile flickered across Miles' face, then vanished. "Something like that."

They talked a bit — about movies, music, small hobbies — nothing deep. Just enough to fill the quiet.

Then Jonah appeared in the doorway.

"Miles."

Miles jumped to his feet.

"Please, don't bother the guests," Jonah said calmly. "You have duties."

"He's not a bo—" Evan started.

"Nonetheless," Jonah cut in gently but firmly, "he has responsibilities." He looked at Miles. "Tend to them."

Miles nodded quickly and hurried out.

Jonah followed a moment later, leaving the living room eerily still.

Evan sat back, watching the fire.

<u>CHAPTER 4</u>

3

Dinner that night felt even grander than the first.

Soft lighting glowed from wrought-iron chandeliers, casting warm halos over polished wood and white linen. The air carried the layered scents of herbs, butter, and roasting meat. Conversations murmured gently.

Evan took his seat and let himself sink into the comfort of it.

Across the room, Marlowe drifted in and out, pausing at tables, exchanging brief words, her presence commanding without effort. Jonah followed her path at a careful distance, quietly attentive, correcting small details before they could become problems.

Rosa moved smoothly between tables, her expression soft, her smile practiced but not unkind. Miles trailed behind her, clearing plates, refilling water glasses, his movements quick and precise. Sam remained near the bar, pouring drinks, his posture relaxed but his eyes alert.

Elena appeared only briefly, stepping out of the kitchen to greet a few guests before vanishing again. Evan wondered, not for the first time, how large her kitchen staff must be. He had yet to hear or see anyone else working back there — no voices, no footsteps, no clatter of pans beyond what drifted faintly through the swinging doors.

The food itself was exceptional.

Perfectly seared salmon, lemon risotto, vegetables roasted just enough to retain their bite. Every bite seemed designed to be savored, not merely eaten.

Ian joined him midway through the meal, looking marginally more rested than before but still subdued.

"I slept for nearly ten hours," Ian admitted quietly. "Woke up feeling like I could go right back."

"Must be something in the air," Evan said.

"Or the fog," Ian replied, half-smiling.

A couple soon joined them — middle-aged, polite, faintly flustered. They explained they'd planned to leave the previous night, but the fallen tree still blocked the road completely.

"Crews were supposed to arrive today," the woman said. "But apparently the fog slowed them down."

"Safety regulations," the man added. "They won't send anyone into conditions like this."

They spoke lightly, but Evan noticed the tension beneath their words — the discomfort of being stranded, even somewhere as pleasant as this.

Conversation drifted easily. Small talk. Travel stories. Compliments about the food. It all felt ordinary.

Normal.

Later, in his room, Evan lay back against the pillows, phone in hand, absently playing a puzzle game. The soft glow of the screen was the only light in the room.

Somewhere beyond the walls, he heard something.

At first, he thought it was the wind.

Then voices.

Low. Indistinct. Close enough to register, too muffled to understand.

Evan paused his game and listened.

The sound ebbed and flowed — quiet conversation, perhaps an argument. He strained to catch words, but nothing resolved clearly. After a moment, curiosity pulled him from bed.

He slipped into the hall.

The lodge was dim and hushed, lit only by soft amber sconces. Shadows pooled along the ceilings. The air smelled faintly of smoke and polished wood.

In the living room, the fireplace still burned weakly — small flames licking at the last of the logs. Evan found a folded blanket draped over the back of one of the couches, wrapped it around his shoulders, and lowered himself into a chair near the hearth.

The warmth seeped into his muscles.

His eyelids drooped.

Somewhere in the half-space between waking and sleep, the voices returned.

Two men. Close. Whispering.

"…needs to be cleaned up," one said.

"That's not my job," the other murmured.

"Yes. It is."

The words blurred together, but the tones sharpened — irritation, urgency, restraint.

The voices sounded like Jonah and Derek.

Evan stirred slightly.

The whispers cut off.

Silence stretched.

"Is someone there?" Jonah's voice called softly.

Evan didn't move. His breathing remained slow, even.

A long pause followed, then quieter murmuring — too faint now to catch. Footsteps retreated. Somewhere deeper in the lodge, a door opened… then closed.

Evan drifted back into sleep.

This time, dreamless.

The next day passed slowly.

Ian barely appeared, emerging only briefly at breakfast before retreating back to his room, pale and subdued.

"Just exhausted," he said. "Feels like I could sleep through the week."

Evan felt it too — a dull heaviness behind his eyes, a lingering lethargy that coffee only partially cut through. He blamed the fog, the stillness, the way time seemed to stretch oddly here.

Determined to shake it off, he changed into running clothes and jogged slow loops around the lodge grounds. The air felt thick in his lungs, but clean. The paths were empty. The silence followed him.

Afterward, he showered, dressed, and spent part of the afternoon shooting pool in the recreation room. His focus drifted, but the familiar rhythm steadied him.

At lunch, something felt... wrong.

It took him a moment to realize what.

The couple from dinner were gone.

Their table sat empty.

He frowned slightly, trying to recall their names — or even their faces. Details slipped through his thoughts like water through open fingers. Brown hair? Gray? He wasn't sure.

He dismissed it.

They must have left early. The road must have cleared.

Still, the unease lingered.

Later, while Jonah was occupied elsewhere, Evan wandered toward the front desk and idly flipped through the brochures laid out across the counter.

Local hiking trails. Scenic overlooks. Whale-watching tours.

From the corner of his eye, something else caught his attention.

The guest log.

Its leather cover lay slightly askew, pages open.

Evan leaned closer.

A full day of entries was missing.

Not torn out — simply… absent. The handwriting jumped abruptly from one date to the next, as though time itself had skipped forward.

He stared.

A presence stirred behind him.

"Did you need something, Mr. Mercer?"

Evan turned.

Marlowe stood there, her expression calm, pleasant, perfectly neutral.

"Oh — no," he said quickly, lifting one of the brochures. "Just looking."

"Very well." Her gaze lingered on his face for a brief moment. "If you need anything at all, just ask."

She walked away, heels silent against the polished floor.

Evan remained where he was, brochure still in hand, pulse racing just a little faster than before.

CHAPTER 5

Evan woke to pale morning light spilling across the ceiling.

For a moment, he lay still, listening to the quiet hush of wind outside his window, the soft creak of the lodge settling in its frame. Everything felt normal. Familiar. Comforting.

He showered, dressed, and headed down for breakfast.

The dining room glowed with warm light. Coffee steamed. Plates clinked softly. Elena's voice drifted from the kitchen, cheerful, bright. The smell of fresh bread, bacon and eggs filled the air, rich and grounding.

Evan ate slowly, savoring every bite. The food tasted even better than he remembered — fuller somehow, deeper. The fruit burst with sweetness. The eggs were impossibly light. Even the coffee seemed richer, smoother, almost velvety on his tongue.

He felt *good*. Rested. Clear.

After breakfast, he stepped outside to jog.

The morning fog had thinned but not disappeared, hanging low between the trees like drifting breath. Sunlight filtered through it in pale shafts, casting soft gold across the gravel paths.

He started his usual circuit around the lodge.

The first lap felt normal.

The second felt... slightly different.

The trail curved where it hadn't before, veering closer to the tree line. He slowed, glancing around. The lodge still stood behind him, solid and comforting. The forest pressed closer ahead.

He shrugged it off and continued.

On the third loop, he noticed the path he normally took had nearly vanished beneath leaf litter and pine needles, while a new trail — narrow but clearly worn — branched off beside it.

That hadn't been there yesterday.

Or had it?

He paused, studying the ground. The dirt was compacted, footprints faint but visible. Not fresh. Not old. Just... there.

A sound drifted through the fog.

Soft. Almost musical.

"Evan."

He stopped.

The voice was faint, distant — carried on the wind. He turned slowly, scanning the trees.

Nothing.

Probably just the breeze through branches, he told himself. Sound carried strangely in fog.

He resumed jogging.

The forest seemed to shift as he moved.

Paths that had been clear moments ago blurred into tangled undergrowth. Others emerged suddenly from the mist — narrow, winding trails that beckoned forward. The fog thinned in places ahead of him, only to thicken behind him, as though closing ranks.

He slowed to a walk.

A figure stood at the edge of visibility, just beyond the nearest veil of fog.

Tall. Slender. Still.

Evan's breath caught.

"Hello?" he called.

The figure didn't answer. Instead, it lifted one arm and gestured — a slow, deliberate motion.

Come.

Evan hesitated.

Every instinct whispered caution, but something else tugged at him — a quiet pull deep in his chest. Not fear. Curiosity. A strange sense of familiarity.

He stepped forward.

The figure retreated.

Always just far enough ahead to remain indistinct.

He followed.

The forest thickened as he moved deeper. Redwood trunks loomed like massive pillars, their bark dark and furrowed. Ferns brushed his legs. The air cooled. Damp earth and moss filled his lungs.

The light shifted.

Colors deepened.

The greens sharpened, glowing with unnatural vibrancy. The browns of bark and soil darkened into rich, velvety tones. Even the fog shimmered faintly, pearlescent and alive.

The world felt *too vivid*.

"Evan," the voice whispered again.

Closer now.

He turned sharply.

Nothing.

When he faced forward again, the figure had vanished.

Unease crept up his spine.

"Hello?" His voice sounded smaller here, swallowed by the towering forest.

A path opened before him — narrow, deliberate, unmistakably shaped by foot traffic.

He followed it.

The trees pressed in tighter. Branches arched overhead, weaving together into a vaulted canopy that swallowed the sky. The fog thickened, coiling between trunks like slow-moving smoke.

Footsteps crunched behind him.

Evan stopped.

They stopped too.

He turned.

A man stood directly behind him.

So close that Evan felt his breath.

He hadn't heard him approach.

The man's face was calm, unreadable. His features were strong, weathered — lines etched by wind and time rather than age. His dark hair hung loose around his shoulders, threaded with subtle beads and leather ties. A vest of animal pelt rested over his shoulders, simple, functional — not ceremonial, not dramatic. Just worn. Real.

Ancient.

The man's eyes held Evan's.

"You don't belong here."

The words sounded inside Evan's skull, not in the air.

The man's lips never moved.

Cold flooded Evan's veins.

Every muscle locked.

His pulse thundered in his ears.

He spun—

BAM!

A violent crack shattered the quiet.

Evan jerked upright in bed, heart slamming against his ribs, lungs dragging in sharp, panicked breaths.

A heavy branch scraped against the outside of his window, driven by a sudden gust of wind. Leaves rattled. Glass trembled.

For a moment, he just sat there, soaked in sweat, chest heaving.

Then he exhaled shakily and collapsed back against the pillows.

Just a dream.

The wind howled softly outside, then slowly settled.

Evan closed his eyes.

Sleep reclaimed him.

And when he woke again later that morning, the dream was already slipping away — dissolving into vague unease, leaving behind nothing more than the faint echo of uneasiness he couldn't quite explain.

The real morning came slowly.

Evan surfaced from sleep feeling heavy, as though he'd spent the night swimming through thick water. His limbs ached faintly, his head dull and clouded. He lay still for several moments, staring at the ceiling, waiting for clarity that never fully arrived.

Whatever he'd been dreaming about slipped away before he could grasp it.

At breakfast, his appetite was gone.

He settled for toast and coffee, nibbling absently while watching the quiet movements of the staff. The dining room felt muted, the bright warmth of previous mornings dulled by the lingering fog beyond the windows.

Afterward, he drifted into the living room and selected a book from the shelves — a local history collection, thick with photographs and faded maps. The cover promised *Legends of the Redwood Coast: Stories, Myths, and Memory.*

He sank into one of the leather chairs near the fireplace, the crackle of the flames the only sound beyond the whisper of turning pages.

Some of the stories were strange.

Old logging accidents. Vanished settlements. Hikers who wandered off marked trails and were never found. Indigenous legends that spoke of forest spirits, tricksters, guardians, watchers. The prose was dry, academic, but something about the repetition of disappearance unsettled him.

He read about 'The Watchers', forest guardian spirits. According to the book, forests were believed to house sentient spirits, protective entities, land guardians. These spirits protected ancient groves, watched over travelers and enforced spiritual balance. He wondered if these were the legends that the kid at the gas station... was his name Caleb... was talking about.

At some point, soft footsteps crossed the rug.

Elena stepped into the room, scanning the shelves. She selected a thick, dog-eared cookbook and hugged it to her chest.

"Elena," Evan said gently. "Do you have a moment?"

Her face brightened instantly. "Of course."

She crossed the room and perched on the arm of the chair beside him.

"That book looks well-loved," he said, nodding at the cookbook.

She laughed. "This one's been with me for years. My grandmother wrote half of them in the margins."

"So the food here..."

"...comes from about three generations of stubborn women who refused to measure anything properly," she finished, grinning.

They both laughed.

"Where do you find all the ingredients?" Evan asked. "Some of it tastes like it came straight out of someone's backyard."

Elena lifted the book slightly. "We get dry goods delivered once a month, the last one came a few days before you did. Meats are bi-monthly, we have a huge walk-in meat locker. And the produce comes from our garden. Derek tends to it, he tends to everything. And the rest is just… practice." She shrugged. "Cooking's like learning a language. Once you understand the rules, you can start bending them."

"Seems like you've mastered it."

She rolled her eyes playfully. "Flattery will get you extra dessert."

Behind her, movement caught Evan's eye.

At the reception desk, a couple stood checking in — a man and a woman, both bundled in light jackets, their posture weary but hopeful. Jonah spoke quietly to them, his tone calm and reassuring. Their responses were indistinct, swallowed by distance.

Evan hadn't even noticed them enter.

Elena followed his gaze and smiled. "New guests."

He nodded absently.

"Well," she said, hopping down, "guess I'd better get cookin'." She started toward the lobby, then paused. "Nice talking to you, Evan."

"Always."

She offered a quick wave before heading off, calling a cheerful greeting to the couple as she passed.

Evan leaned back in his chair.

Miles stood nearby, folding the small blanket Evan had used the other night. Their eyes met briefly — a flicker of recognition, a ghost of a smile — before Jonah's voice cut across the room.

"Miles."

Miles straightened instantly and crossed to the desk. Jonah beckoned him toward the couple, and Miles nodded, collecting their bags and leading them toward the stairs.

Something tugged at Evan's memory.

The moment felt familiar.

Yes, Jonah had called Miles over when Evan himself had arrived. That wasn't it. This felt... other. As though he'd watched the same interaction play out from Miles' vantage point.

He shook his head and returned his attention to the book.

Still, the words blurred.

His thoughts wandered.

He'd seen a handful of people checking in since his arrival. He remembered their faces vaguely — flashes of smiles, passing greetings, murmured hellos over meals.

But he hadn't seen anyone leave.

During his morning jogs, he'd noticed cars in the parking lot. Some were gone later. Others appeared in their place.

Guests came and went, he reasoned. He just hadn't been paying attention.

That explanation settled uneasily in his mind.

Ian had barely come downstairs anymore.

He'd still appear for meals, pale and subdued, eating slowly before retreating back upstairs. The easy humor Evan had first encountered had dulled into something distant, as though Ian were perpetually fighting exhaustion.

Evan frowned.

By mid-afternoon, concern outweighed hesitation.

He crossed the dining room and found Rosa near the kitchen, arranging freshly folded napkins into neat stacks.

"Mrs. Calder?" he asked softly.

She turned, her lined face brightening at once. "Yes, dear?"

"I was wondering…" He hesitated. "My friend Ian — he hasn't been feeling well. Would it be alright if I took him up some soup?"

Her expression softened. "Of course. Poor thing's been worn thin."

She ladled steaming broth into a porcelain bowl, adding thick slices of bread and a small plate of fruit.

"Thank you," Evan said.

"Such a thoughtful young man," she murmured fondly patting his cheek with her soft motherly hands.

He balanced the tray carefully and headed upstairs.

Ian's door was cracked open.

Evan knocked gently. "Ian?"

No response.

He pushed the door wider.

The room was dim, curtains drawn. Ian lay sprawled across the bed, still in his pajamas, breathing slow and deep. His skin looked pale, almost translucent in the muted light.

"Hey," Evan said quietly. "Brought you some soup."

Ian stirred, blinking groggily. "What time is it?" he asked stretching.

"Afternoon."

"Feels like I just laid down," Ian muttered.

"You've been sleeping a lot."

Ian gave a weak chuckle. "Guess I needed it."

Evan set the tray on the bedside table. "Eat what you can."

"I will," Ian promised. "Thanks."

Evan lingered a moment, then nodded and slipped back into the hallway.

As he descended the stairs, unease curled low in his stomach.

That night, he barely slept.

CHAPTER 6

Evan woke before his alarm.

For a moment, he lay still, listening.

The lodge was never truly silent — there was always the faint hum of electricity in the walls, the soft ticking of cooling pipes, the distant creak of wood settling. But beneath it all now, there seemed to be something else. A low, almost imperceptible whisper, like wind passing through a narrow space.

He sat up, the sensation fading as quickly as it had come.

Just the building, he told himself.

After dressing, he headed downstairs, grabbed a piece of toast and a mug of coffee, and stepped outside into the morning fog.

The air was cool and wet, heavy with the scent of pine and damp earth. The world beyond the lodge was muted, edges softened, the towering redwoods reduced to pale silhouettes that vanished into mist overhead.

It felt like running inside a cloud.

He stretched, adjusted his jacket, and started his jog.

The gravel path crunched beneath his boots as he made his first loop around the lodge. The familiar curve near the western wing, the slight incline near the garden beds, the narrow stretch beside the treeline — everything was exactly as he remembered.

The second lap, he noticed the curve near the western wing felt...
longer.

Not dramatically so. Just enough that his internal sense of timing
flagged it.

He slowed slightly, glancing around.

The lodge still stood solidly to his right, its windows dark and
reflective. The forest pressed close on the left, fog threading
between the trunks. The path curved gently forward, vanishing into
haze.

Probably just my perception, he thought. Fog does that.

He kept running.

On the third lap, the narrow stretch beside the treeline was gone.

In its place, the path widened, splitting into two faint trails — one
continuing along the lodge, the other drifting subtly toward the
forest.

Evan slowed to a walk.

He stood there for a long moment, staring at the fork.

This wasn't right.

He was certain of that.

He had run this route every morning since arriving. The rhythm of
it was already locked into his body — the turns, the pacing, the
landmarks. There had never been a split here.

He stepped forward, crouching to examine the ground.

The soil was compacted. Leaves were pressed flat. Pine needles were scattered thinly, disturbed recently enough that they hadn't fully settled back into place.

Someone — or something — had used this path.

He straightened, gaze drifting toward the forest trail.

It curved gently out of sight, swallowed by fog and ferns.

A faint unease brushed his spine.

Not fear.

More like… hesitation.

The sense of standing at the edge of a thought he wasn't sure he wanted to finish.

After a moment, he shook his head and continued along the lodge-side trail.

Better not to wander.

The next two loops passed without incident, though the forest felt closer than before. The fog thickened, thinning unpredictably, revealing sudden glimpses of immense tree trunks before closing again.

Then he heard it.

"Evan."

The voice was soft. But authoritative.

He slowed, breath fogging in front of his face.

"Hello?" he called.

Only silence answered.

The forest stood motionless.

Probably the wind, he told himself.

Sound carried strangely in places like this. The fog, the trees, the way air folded around uneven terrain — it could twist echoes into something that almost sounded like speech.

Almost.

He resumed jogging.

A few minutes later, he heard it again.

"Evan."

Closer this time.

He stopped.

His pulse raced faster.

"Is someone there?"

Nothing.

But as he turned, scanning the fog, he caught movement — a flicker of motion between the trunks. Something tall and slender, slipping behind a massive redwood.

He stared.

The forest returned his gaze, impassive.

Probably another guest, he reasoned. Early riser, like him. Maybe someone exploring.

Still, he didn't see anyone emerge.

When he resumed his jog, the paths began to feel… wrong.

Not dramatically. Not obviously.

But small inconsistencies stacked quietly atop one another.

A boulder he remembered passing on the right appeared on the left.

A fallen log he swore had been moss-covered yesterday now looked freshly exposed.

The slope near the back garden flattened out, then subtly steepened again.

Each change alone meant nothing.

Together, they whispered. Almost shouted.

By the time he completed his circuit, the lodge felt farther away than it should have been.

He slowed to a walk, heart thudding just a little too hard for the effort he'd expended.

Standing near the rear of the property, he turned in a slow circle.

Fog drifted between the trees, reforming constantly, reshaping the world. Trails appeared, vanished, bent and folded in on themselves.

The forest no longer looked like a collection of objects — trees, brush, earth — but a single shifting mass.

A presence.

Watching.

No.

He shook his head sharply.

You're tired. That's all.

He started back toward the lodge.

Halfway there, he caught another glimpse of movement.

This time, he was sure.

Someone stood between two trees about fifty yards away.

They were mostly obscured by fog, but he could make out the rough outline of a human figure — upright, still, facing him.

"Hey!" he called.

The figure did not move.

Evan hesitated, then took a cautious step forward.

The fog thickened.

When it thinned again, the space between the trees was empty.

A chill crept across his shoulders.

By the time he reached the lodge, his easy morning rhythm was gone. He felt wired, alert, his senses straining for patterns, explanations, logic.

That afternoon, he jogged again.

And again.

By early evening, he had circled the lodge more times than he could easily count.

Running kept him awake. Kept the heaviness from pulling him under. Without it, he found himself drifting — nodding off in chairs, losing track of time, sinking into a sleep that felt too deep, too thick, like falling through warm water.

So he ran.

And the more laps he took, the more the forest seemed to notice.

Shadows lingered just beyond the corners of his vision.

Whispers skimmed across the edges of hearing, never quite resolving into words.

Paths bent. Shifted. Stretched in ways that made his sense of direction wobble.

At times, the trail appeared to lead somewhere new — a narrow opening between trunks, a subtle turn he didn't remember, a gentle slope dipping into deeper fog.

Each time, he felt the same soft internal nudge.

Come.

Each time, he ignored it.

Fatigue, he told himself. Dehydration. Overexertion. Sensory distortion from repetitive motion.

He went back inside.

He ate.

He read.

He made small talk in the common areas, exchanged nods and polite smiles with other guests, listened to fragments of conversation drift past him like loose leaves.

Normal things.

Comforting things.

Yet even sitting near the fire, a book open but unread in his hands, his attention kept drifting toward the windows.

The forest pressed close to the glass, a wall of dark trunks and pale fog. Sometimes it felt like the trees leaned in just slightly, as if listening.

He began spending long stretches simply watching.

Not searching.

Not expecting.

Just... waiting.

His fingers worked his padlock absently, the familiar motions grounding, steady. The gentle click of the pins sliding into place marked time more reliably than the clock on the wall.

There was a feeling he couldn't quite shake.

Like forgetting an appointment you never remembered making.

A low, persistent tension in the back of his mind. The certainty that something had been scheduled, arranged, anticipated — and that he was late.

Or worse.

That he was being waited for.

At odd moments, the sensation sharpened, becoming almost physical. A prickle between his shoulder blades. The subtle awareness of being observed.

Each time he lifted his gaze, there was no one there.

No movement. No figures. No sound.

Just fog and trees and glass.

By evening, exhaustion finally overtook him.

But even as he drifted toward sleep, the sense remained — faint but insistent.

Something out there was trying to get his attention.

And for reasons he couldn't fully articulate, Evan kept ignoring it.

CHAPTER 7

Evan slept late. He was exhausted after a full day of jogging — the rhythm of the trails, the shifting fog, the forest pressing close — all of it had left him drained.

This morning, he took a long, hot bath, letting the warmth soak into his shoulders and ease the tight muscles along his spine. He dressed in his most comfortable blue jeans, a soft t-shirt, and a warm hoodie. He tied his shoes slowly, enjoying the small ritual, when a soft knock came at the door.

"Mr. Mercer?"

"Come on in, Miles," Evan called out, straightening as the door opened. "And it's Evan," he reminded him.

Miles froze for a moment, then corrected himself. "Right, Evan," he said, flushing slightly.

Evan gave him a faint smile. "It's fine. How's it going?"

Miles shifted, hands in his pockets. "Mr. Ho — I mean, Ian, is staying in his room today," he said finally. "But you're free to visit if you like."

"Thanks. I'll probably take lunch with him," Evan said. "Could you pass that along?"

Miles nodded, then headed down the hall, and Evan made his way toward the stairs.

The common areas were quiet but alive with small activity. Jonah wasn't at the desk — likely attending to some early administrative task — but Derek was outside on a ladder, sweeping pine needles from the gutters. Sam, Rosa, and Elena were clustered at the bar; Rosa sat with her hands folded in her lap, Sam leaned behind the counter with a mug of coffee, and Elena stood next to Rosa, resting a hand lightly on the back of her chair.

Evan approached the bar. "Sam," he said, "do you have any of that Veranda Blend? The Starbucks one — the blonde roast?"

"Sure do," Sam replied with a grin, pouring fresh grounds into the machine. "Not sure you're ready for this much caffeine first thing, though."

"Trust me," Evan said with a small smile. "I need it."

He turned to Elena. "What's on the menu today?"

Elena tapped a finger against her lips in thought. "Let's see… I made a roasted vegetable frittata with caramelized onions and Gruyère. I also prepped a cinnamon apple compote that goes well with it. And Rosa baked that rosemary focaccia you like."

Rosa smiled, eyes warm. "I added a little olive tapenade to the focaccia — not too much, just enough to bring out the rosemary. Thought you might appreciate that."

Evan leaned against the bar, watching them work, enjoying the rhythm of conversation, the casual camaraderie. "Elena, I've been meaning to ask… do you have a favorite way to make your compote? I tried something similar once, but it didn't taste quite right."

"Oh, it's simple," Elena said, leaning forward. "Slice the apples thin, sprinkle a quarter cup of brown sugar over them, a dash of cinnamon, and a tablespoon of butter. Cook slowly over medium heat until they're soft but still hold a little shape. A touch of lemon juice brightens it at the end. That's it."

Evan nodded. "I think I undercooked mine last time. That's probably why it was mushy."

Rosa chimed in, "For the bread, I usually mix a quarter cup of olive tapenade directly into the dough before the final rise. It gives the flavor depth without overpowering the rosemary. Works surprisingly well with roasted garlic, too."

They swapped a few more tips — techniques for caramelizing onions, how to get the perfect egg consistency for frittatas, even a small debate over whether Gruyère or fontina was better for melting. The conversation felt casual, grounding, almost comforting in the midst of everything else.

Sam handed Evan a steaming mug of coffee. He thanked him and left a tip on the counter, taking the cup into the living room. He popped in a DVD — *The Pest*, something light and ridiculous — and settled into the couch. The mug warmed his hands as he took the first sip of the smooth roast.

Moments later, Miles appeared and dropped into the chair next to him.

"Thought you weren't supposed to socialize with guests," Evan said with a smirk.

"Jonah gave me the morning off," Miles replied. "Thought I'd watch a movie."

"Want me to change it?"

"No, I've never seen this one," Miles said, shoulders relaxing.

The movie played quietly in the background, dialogue and laughter filling the room. Miles eventually leaned back, hands behind his head.

"So… what do you actually do?" he asked, glancing at Evan. "You travel a lot… I mean, for work."

Evan explained in layman's terms, careful not to get too technical. "I handle systems engineering. Mostly infrastructure, networks, software that keeps things running."

Miles nodded slowly. "Sounds… complicated."

"It has its moments," Evan said. "I like it. Makes sense once you know how it all fits together."

"What about you?" Evan asked. "Did you want to work here?"

Miles shrugged. "My uncle wanted me here. Said it would be good for me. Thought I'd learn responsibility."

Evan raised an eyebrow. "And… do you?"

Miles hesitated, then gave a small, honest smile. "I guess. Some days. But I like it when it's quiet, when no one's needing something every second. Makes the hours pass easier."

"School?" Evan pressed gently. "College plans? Anything you'd rather be doing?"

Miles leaned back, thinking. "I don't know. Maybe something outdoors. Forestry, environmental science. Something not stuck inside all day. But… yeah, my uncle said it's best to learn first, live later."

They fell into a rhythm, watching the movie, sharing stories about favorite classes, teachers, small personal victories. Evan found himself asking questions he didn't normally ask anyone. He discovered Miles could bake a mean chocolate chip cookie, enjoyed sketching landscapes, and had a knack for remembering tiny details about people he barely knew.

At one point, Evan glanced at the living room window. The forest was still there, looming, fog drifting between trunks, but he felt… calmer, grounded.

He sipped coffee, listened to Miles' quiet observations about the world, and tucked away details for later. The forest and lodge felt distant in those moments, like a world paused while he existed in the safety of conversation, laughter, and warmth.

And yet, even in comfort, a subtle, nagging awareness lingered at the back of his mind: something beyond the walls was still watching. Learning. Waiting.

The movie rolled on, the chaotic antics on screen keeping both men entertained in quiet bursts of laughter. Eventually, Miles stretched and glanced at the clock. "My break is over, I'll be seeing you Mr. Me – uh, Evan." he said.

Evan nodded. "Yeah. I'm going to go grab lunch for Ian and I." He set his mug down and rose, heading for the dining area.

Rosa appeared just as he was gathering plates. "Heading up to Ian's?" she asked, a gentle smile softening her sharp features.

"Yes," Evan said. "Want to come help me carry it?"

Rosa chuckled. "Of course. Someone needs to make sure you don't spill it on the stairs."

They moved quickly through the lodge, the aroma of fresh bread, roasted vegetables, and lightly spiced chicken drifting through the hallways. Evan loaded the tray with sandwiches, fruit, and a thermos of soup. Rosa grabbed the cutlery and drinks.

At Ian's door, Rosa knocked lightly. "Lunch is here," she said.

Ian's muffled voice called from inside. "Thanks! Just a minute."

When he opened the door, Evan noticed the faint flush in Ian's cheeks, and the small blanket tucked around his shoulders. The two men exchanged a quick grin. "Ready?" Evan asked.

Ian nodded, motioning for them to enter. He cleared a small table beside his bed, carefully balancing the tray as Evan and Rosa set everything down. Soon, the two men were sitting cross-legged, plates balanced on their knees.

As they ate, Ian pointed out his portable video game console on the dresser that he always carried. "You play?" he asked.

Evan raised an eyebrow. "Haven't in years, but why not?"

Minutes passed as they took turns racing, tapping, and laughing at the game's absurdities. Evan guffawed when Ian pulled off a particularly tricky move, laughing at the boyish competitiveness. The food was barely touched at first, but by the time they paused, the sandwiches had disappeared and the fruit bowls were half-empty.

Rosa appeared at the door again, a small tray of hot cocoa and chocolate chip cookies in hand. "I thought you might need a little dessert," she said. "Still warm from the oven."

Evan grinned. "Perfect." As Ian's eyes lit up. They sipped cocoa, the warmth and sweetness settling into their bellies, laughter fading into quiet comfort.

When the last crumbs had been eaten, Ian stretched and set his controller aside. "I'm going to take a bath. Be down for dinner."

"Alright," Evan said, standing. "I'll make sure everything's tidy."

He punched Ian's shoulder gently, and gave him a quick nod. "I'll be downstairs."

Evan stepped back into the hallway, tray cleared, and made his way down to the lounge. The quiet warmth of the room greeted him, the movie's DVD menu still repeating on the screen. For a moment, the lodge felt normal again, cozy even. But as he replaced the disk into its case and put it back, he couldn't help but glance toward the windows, where the fog pressed against the glass, dark and silent, waiting.

CHAPTER 8

Evan went back upstairs and decided to take a nap. Much like Ian, he felt dog tired today.

The exhaustion sat heavy in his limbs, the kind that made even simple movements feel deliberate, effortful. His body sank gratefully into the mattress as soon as he lay down.

The dream came quickly.

Too quickly.

He stood in the forest again.

Not standing — *placed*. As if he had been set down precisely where something expected him to be.

The trees were wrong — not twisted, not monstrous, just subtly off. Their trunks leaned at shallow, unnatural angles. The moss on their bark pulsed faintly, like something breathing beneath skin. The path beneath his feet bent gently, as if curving away from him even as he walked forward.

A faint pressure hummed in the air, the uncomfortable sensation of being inside a sealed room where no walls were visible.

Voices whispered.

Not words. Not quite. More like fragments — clipped syllables, overlapping murmurs, half-formed intentions that brushed against his mind without fully landing.

They seemed to slide across his thoughts rather than enter them, skimming the surface like fingertips trailing through water.

He turned in place, searching.

The forest shifted.

Not violently. Not dramatically. Just… rearranged itself.

Landmarks slid a few feet sideways. Trees subtly traded places. The curve of the trail smoothed, then sharpened again, never quite settling.

He became acutely aware that he was not alone.

Something unseen moved parallel to him, close enough that he felt its presence like pressure against his ribs. He couldn't hear footsteps. Couldn't see movement. Only the certainty that if he reached out, his hand would meet something solid.

His skin prickled with the instinctive warning of proximity, the animal knowledge of being hunted or studied.

The whispers swelled.

For a moment, a phrase surfaced clearly:

Go.

His chest tightened.

"Where?" he said aloud, his voice sounding thin and distant.

The sound didn't echo. It simply vanished, absorbed by the moss and bark.

The forest seemed to lean in.

Branches dipped. The path narrowed. Even the air thickened, heavy in his lungs.

The ground softened beneath his boots.

The sensation was wrong — not sinking, not collapsing, but yielding, as though the forest itself were making room for him.

He jerked awake with a sharp inhale.

His heart hammered, his shirt damp with sweat. Late afternoon light filtered through the curtains, casting long shadows across the room.

For a few seconds, he remained perfectly still, half-expecting the walls to tilt, the floor to breathe.

Evan sat up slowly, grounding himself: the bed. The walls. The dresser. The door.

Solid. Familiar. Obedient to physics.

Reality reassembled piece by piece.

Still, unease clung stubbornly to his skin.

After splashing cold water on his face, he pulled on his hoodie and stepped outside.

The chill bit pleasantly, clearing the fog from his head, but not the weight from his thoughts.

The air was cool, carrying the scent of wet pine and distant earth. Evan walked slowly at first, then gradually lengthened his stride, following the familiar perimeter trail that circled the lodge grounds.

Each step felt like reclaiming territory from the dream.

The forest was peaceful — deceptively so.

Birdsong filtered through the branches. Wind stirred fallen needles across the dirt path.

Somewhere in the distance, water trickled over rock.

Everything looked ordinary. Which somehow made it worse.

Yet the dream lingered, overlaying the real world like a translucent shadow.

He found himself scanning the trees for subtle wrongness, half-expecting them to shift if he looked too long.

He completed one full loop without incident, his mind gradually settling. Halfway through his second lap, he slowed as he approached the east wing of the lodge.

His pace became deliberate, cautious, his senses tuned outward.

One of the windows stood partially open.

Voices drifted out.

Not loudly. Just enough.

"…deep enough sleep…"

Evan froze.

The words slid neatly into the hollow space the dream had carved.

He shifted his weight carefully, pretending to adjust his boot, angling himself closer without stepping directly beneath the window.

His pulse thudded loudly in his ears, each beat threatening to give him away.

The voices were muffled, overlapping — three people, he thought. Two men, one woman. The woman's voice was smoother, calmer. One man rougher, clipped. One quieter, tighter.

"...won't remember..."

"...risk if—"

"...can't rush—"

The words slipped away before he could piece them together.

Fragments without context, sharp enough to wound, too incomplete to explain.

He straightened slowly and resumed walking, heart thudding uncomfortably in his chest.

"Deep enough sleep".

The phrase echoed far louder in his mind than it had aloud.

He completed the rest of the loop with forced steadiness, but when he returned to the same stretch, something made him glance up.

Marlowe stood at her office window.

Not leaning. Not pretending to work.

Just… watching.

Their eyes met.

For a fraction of a second, her expression was unreadable — not startled, not guilty. Simply assessing.

Then she turned away.

Unease prickled along Evan's spine.

The moment replayed itself, frame by frame, in his thoughts.

He took several more steps before he noticed another presence.

Derek stood at an upstairs window, partially obscured by the frame, his broad shoulders unmistakable. He wasn't cleaning. Wasn't moving.
he too, was just watching.

Evan's stomach tightened.

The symmetry of it felt intentional.

He finished the lap and returned inside, pulse still elevated, thoughts spinning in overlapping loops.

Dinner was already underway.

The lodge dining room glowed warmly, lamplight reflecting off polished wood and glass. Plates clinked softly. Low conversation hummed between staff.

Normal. Domestic. Carefully ordinary.

Evan filled a plate with roasted chicken, potatoes, and green beans, then took a seat at the far table.

Normally, he would have joined in. Listened. Asked questions. Shared small observations.

Tonight, he stayed quiet.

Instead, he watched.

Jonah stood behind the bar, posture relaxed, laughter easy — but Evan noticed how his gaze tracked movement across the room, always aware of who stood where.

Sam poured drinks, smooth and efficient, but his eyes flicked often toward Marlowe's closed office door.

Elena moved briskly between kitchen and table, her expression soft, but tension sat tight in her shoulders.

Rosa fussed over plates, her warmth genuine, yet her eyes held a quiet concern she hadn't worn before.

Derek leaned against the far wall, arms crossed, scanning the room like a sentry.

And Marlowe did not join them.

Evan chewed slowly, mind dissecting every gesture, every glance, every subtle pause.

Who knew what?

Who didn't?

Was it only the three?

Or was everyone part of something he simply couldn't see yet?

The lodge felt different now.

Not hostile.

Not dangerous.

But… layered.

Like a stage set where he could finally see the edges of the backdrop.

He finished his meal, returned his plate, and excused himself early, claiming fatigue.

Upstairs, alone once more, he locked his door and leaned back against it for a moment, breathing slowly.

For the first time since his arrival, the sense of being watched did not fade when he laid his head on his pillow.

CHAPTER 9

Evan woke slowly.

Not abruptly. Not from fear or noise or the echo of a dream. Just… gradually, drifting upward through layers of sleep until awareness settled gently back into place.

For a few seconds, he lay still, staring at the ceiling, cataloging the quiet. The soft hiss of the radiator. The distant murmur of water moving somewhere in the lodge's hidden plumbing. The faint rustle of branches brushing against the exterior wall.

Something felt off.

Not wrong, exactly. Just… weighted. Like waking with the sense that a thought had been interrupted, a thread dropped mid-sentence.

Unease lingered beneath his calm, faint but persistent.

He frowned slightly, searching his memory.

Nothing surfaced at first. Only a vague impression of pressure, of being watched, of something unfinished.

Then it snapped back into focus.

The forest.

The voices.

Go.

The overheard conversation.

Deep enough sleep.

Marlowe at the window.

Derek, watching from above.

Evan exhaled slowly and pushed himself upright, running a hand through his hair. The room looked the same as it always had — tidy, neutral, quietly comfortable — but now it felt staged. Like a set rebuilt overnight to look reassuring.

He swung his legs over the side of the bed and sat there for a moment, letting the weight of the mattress pull at him, grounding himself before standing.

His body still ached faintly, the deep exhaustion of accumulated strain. Jogging was out of the question today. Even walking felt like it would require intention.

Still, the urge to move pressed at him.

To get outside.

To clear his head.

After a quick shower and fresh clothes, he stepped into the hallway and made his way downstairs. The lodge was unusually quiet, voices muted, footsteps distant. When he pushed open the main doors, cool air washed over him, carrying the scent of damp earth and pine resin.

And he stopped short.

The fog was gone.

Not entirely — a fine, silvery mist still threaded through the forest, but it no longer pressed close, no longer swallowed distance. Sunlight filtered through the towering trunks in long, luminous beams, illuminating drifting particles like floating gold dust. The forest floor glowed in patches of soft green and honey. Dew clung to moss and needles, catching the light.

It was... beautiful.

Unquestionably so.

Evan stepped forward, drawn by the unexpected clarity. The trail lay before him in crisp detail, each curve visible, each stone sharply outlined. The oppressive enclosure he'd grown accustomed to had lifted, leaving space, air, openness.

For a moment, the unease loosened its grip.

He walked slowly, breathing deeply, letting the serenity soak into him. The forest seemed transformed — no longer looming, no longer whispering. Birds flitted between branches. Sun-warmed bark released a clean, resinous scent. Somewhere nearby, water moved lazily over smooth stone.

This was the kind of place people escaped to.

The kind of place brochures were made of.

He reached for his phone.

Framed the sunlight cutting through the trees. The pale mist coiling delicately around massive trunks. The path ahead, glowing softly.

He snapped several photos, adjusting angles, stepping backward for a wider shot — and frowned.

He framed the lodge itself, stepping back until the building sat perfectly between two towering firs. The angle was ideal — warm light washing over the wood, fog drifting just enough to soften the edges, the windows catching the sun like quiet eyes.

He raised the phone and snapped the picture.

Then frowned.

A small point of light hovered near the roofline.

He adjusted his stance and took another.

The light remained.

Not a reflection. Not lens flare. Too sharp. Too precise.

Evan slowly lowered the phone, glanced up at the lodge with his naked eye.

Nothing.

No visible fixtures. No glint. No reflective surface where the light should have been.

He lifted the phone again.

The point of light burned steadily in the frame.

His pulse sped up.

He shifted sideways, changing the angle.

The light moved with the building.

He zoomed in.

The glow sharpened into a tiny, focused dot — faintly violet, faintly red, tucked into the shadow beneath an eave.

Infrared.

The realization settled coldly into place.

His gaze lifted, scanning the building while the phone remained raised.

Another faint light.

Then another.

Along the upper trim. Near window frames. Tucked into corners. Hidden where no casual glance would ever land.

Invisible to the naked eye.

Perfectly visible through his camera.

Cameras.

Not obvious ones. Not security-grade installations meant to deter trespassers.

Carefully concealed.

Thoughtfully placed.

Evan slowly rotated in place.

The forest path.

The outer buildings.

The edge of the tree line.

Nothing.

He turned back toward the lodge, there they were again.

His breath slowed, deliberate, controlled.

He lowered the phone and stared at the lodge again — at its warm windows, its welcoming posture, its careful symmetry.

A staged haven.

A controlled environment.

He slipped the phone back into his pocket, suddenly conscious of the open air, the visibility of his body in space.

The sunlight felt performative now.

The mist, curated.

The peace, constructed.

He finished the loop without incident, but the serenity no longer soothed.

It observed.

By the time he returned inside, late breakfast was winding down.

The dining room was sparsely occupied — a few solitary figures scattered across tables, eating quietly. Rosa passed through carrying a tray of empty dishes. Elena disappeared into the kitchen. Sam wiped down the bar, humming softly.

No one paid Evan much attention.

He filled a plate with scrambled eggs, toast, and fruit, poured himself coffee, and chose a small table near the window. As he ate, he studied the room, his gaze drifting from person to person, noting posture, expression, movement.

Everyone seemed... calm.

Relaxed.

Too relaxed.

The previous night's tension had evaporated, replaced with a carefully curated peace.

When he finished, Evan carried his plate back and wandered into the living room.

Sunlight streamed through the tall windows, casting warm patches across the furniture. The fire crackled softly, low and steady. He retrieved the thick blanket he'd used before, wrapping it around his shoulders before sinking into the deepest, softest chair near the hearth.

The chair nearly swallowed him.

Its high back and wide arms formed a cocoon, shielding him from the doorway, turning his focus inward, toward warmth and quiet. He tucked his feet beneath the blanket and let himself relax, eyes drifting toward the flames.

Minutes passed.

Maybe more.

He might have dozed, or simply hovered in that comfortable limbo between waking and sleep.

Movement beyond the window caught his attention.

Outside, near the tree line, Derek stood facing Jonah.

Their conversation wasn't audible, but their body language spoke volumes.

Jonah's posture was tight, shoulders drawn slightly inward, hands clasped loosely in front of him. He looked smaller somehow. Less certain.

Derek stood broad and solid, his stance wide, one hand gesturing sharply as he spoke. His movements were clipped, authoritative.

Evan watched, unsettled.

This was… wrong.

Jonah had always carried quiet authority. Not domineering, but steady — the gravitational center of the lodge's social orbit. Derek, by contrast, had moved through the background, efficient, silent, deferential.

Now, the dynamic had inverted.

Jonah nodded once. Twice.

Derek shook his head.

Jonah tried again, palms lifting slightly in what looked like appeal.

Derek's response was swift. Final.

After a tense pause, Jonah lowered his gaze.

Derek turned and walked away, his strides purposeful, unhesitating, leaving Jonah standing alone.

For a long moment, Jonah didn't move.

He simply stood there, shoulders slumped, staring at the ground.

Then he straightened, squared his posture, and headed back inside.

But something about the set of his shoulders felt forced.

As though he were stepping back into a role.

Evan tightened his grip on the blanket, unease settling deep in his chest.

The pieces were shifting.

And he could finally see the seams.

CHAPTER 10

Evan retreated to his room with careful composure, closing the door behind him as softly as possible.

The moment the latch settled, his breath left him in a slow, controlled exhale.

The image of those pinpricks of light still burned in his mind. Too precise. Too deliberate.

He stood near the center of the room, phone loose in his hand, staring at the familiar furnishings — the bed, the dresser, the armchair, the mirror mounted beside the bathroom door. Nothing looked out of place.

Slowly, casually, he raised his phone as if opening a game.

He swept the camera across the room.

A faint violet dot winked into view near the ceiling corner.

His chest tightened.

He panned lower.

Another.

Near the bed frame.

Another near the window trim.

Then two more — one tucked behind the wardrobe edge, another buried in the shadow beneath the desk.

Six.

At least six.

His pulse thudded.

He stepped closer to the mirror, angling the phone just slightly.

A single, dim point of infrared glimmered from behind the glass.

A hidden camera.

Watching his reflection.

Every angle. Every movement. No blind spots.

Evan lowered the phone slowly, the room suddenly feeling much smaller than it had moments ago.

So he tested the rest of the lodge.

Not openly. Not obviously.

In the hallways, he pretended to text while his camera scanned doorframes and ceiling seams.

In the stairwell, he paused to stretch, casually lifting the phone as if checking the time.

In the dining room, he angled the screen toward decorative beams and wall sconces.

The results were chilling.

Lights bloomed everywhere.

Corners. Vents. Beams. Hidden recesses in carved wood.

The lodge wasn't just monitored.

It was *instrumented*.

Every common space. Every hallway. Every gathering area.

The living room alone contained nearly a dozen.

By the time Evan sank into one of the plush chairs near the fireplace, his thoughts felt like a swarm of insects.

This wasn't hospitality.

This wasn't security.

This was observation.

Control.

"What the hell is this place..." he murmured under his breath.

"Talking to yourself again?"

Ian's voice cut gently through the spiral.

Evan looked up — and froze.

Ian stood in the doorway, looking better than he had since Evan arrived.

Color had returned to his face. His posture was upright, alert. His eyes clear.

"You look…" Evan started, then stopped, recalibrated. "You look good."

Ian grinned. "I feel good. Finally. Whatever bug I had seems to have burned itself out."

Relief surged through Evan, sharp and sudden enough to knock the cameras from his thoughts entirely.

"That's great," he said honestly, standing. "Seriously."

They spent the next few hours together.

They started with pool.

Neither of them cared much about winning. The game gave their hands something to do while their minds stayed alert, conversation drifting between harmless topics — travel, bad job sites, equipment failures, ridiculous client requests.

Normal talk.

Safe talk.

Only gradually did the edge creep in.

"Ever walk into a site and everything looks perfect," Evan said casually, chalking his cue, "but your gut says someone worked way too hard to make it look that way?"

Ian studied the table, then shrugged. "Yeah. That's when I start looking for what I'm *not* supposed to notice."

Evan nodded. "Over-clean installs. Redundant backups. Too much coverage."

Ian lined up his shot, paused. "Nobody wastes resources unless they're hiding a liability."

The ball dropped cleanly into the corner pocket.

"Exactly," Evan said.

They let the silence stretch.

Later, over chess, the tension sharpened.

Ian played aggressively, pushing Evan into defense earlier than usual. Evan adapted, countering with slow, precise maneuvers, trading space for control.

"Ever feel like a system's steering you toward certain decisions?" Evan asked, eyes on the board. "Not forcing. Just... narrowing the options."

Ian exhaled softly through his nose. "All the time. Good design does that. Bad design pretends it doesn't."

"Which is worse?"

Ian considered. "The kind that convinces you the choice was yours."

Evan shifted a bishop.

"Check."

Ian stared at the board, then smiled faintly. "Yeah. That tracks."

They watched an action movie after — something loud, violent, uncomplicated. Explosions, car chases, predictable heroics. The kind of film that required no emotional investment.

Perfect cover.

Evan let the sound fill the room while he studied the reflections in the darkened windows. Staff moved occasionally in the background, quiet, efficient, unobtrusive.

Too unobtrusive.

"They run a tight operation," Evan said mildly.

Ian didn't look away from the screen. "You noticed."

"Hard not to."

A pause.

"Efficient doesn't mean harmless," Ian added.

"No," Evan agreed. "Sometimes it just means practiced."

After dinner, they had a glass of whiskey.

Warmth settled low in Evan's chest, loosening his shoulders without dulling his awareness. The fire crackled nearby, shadows shifting lazily across the walls.

Ian swirled his glass. "You planning on sticking around long?"

"Not sure," Evan said honestly.

Ian nodded slowly. "Yeah. That makes sense."

They drank.

The quiet between them felt different now. Not awkward. Not forced.

Companionable.

But braced.

"Sometimes," Ian said after a while, "you can feel when a site is… off. Even if you can't explain why."

Evan glanced at him. "Yeah."

Ian met his gaze. "Trust that feeling."

Evan nodded once. "I always do."

They parted not long after.

No handshakes. No overt promises.

Just a shared understanding carried silently between them.

And for the first time since arriving at the lodge, Evan didn't feel completely alone inside his own head.

Evan left the lodge early the next morning.

Not jogging.

Not strolling.

Wandering — deliberately unstructured.

He moved beyond the perimeter trails, letting the trees swallow him.

The farther he went, the quieter everything became.

Until his boot caught.

He stumbled, catching himself on a low branch.

A root, he thought.

Then frowned.

He crouched, brushing pine needles aside.

A cable.

Thin. Dark. Almost invisible against soil and shadow.

He traced it carefully, eyes following its path.

It vanished into the earth.

Then he saw another.

And another.

Looking up, he noticed branches that looked... wrong.

Too straight.

Too uniform.

Lines disguised as nature.

The forest was wired.

A perimeter.

A net.

He wandered back toward the lodge, heart hammering.

The parking lot came into view.

And stopped him cold.

Fewer cars.

He stared.

Counted.

Recounted.

"How long have I been here…?"

The question felt suddenly heavy.

Inside, the dining room confirmed it.

Empty seats.

Tables that had once been occupied now unused.

No new faces.

Just missing ones.

He wandered over to the check-in desk again, picked up a brochure at random, and glanced at the guest ledger again.

More dates gone.

Blank stretches.

Time erased.

"Seriously, how long have I been here?" he wondered to himself.

Derek's voice cut in calmly.

"Find what you were looking for?"

Evan nearly flinched and his eyes flew back to the brochure in his hands.

He turned, schooling his expression. "Just browsing."

Derek smiled faintly.

But his eyes were sharp.

Evaluating.

Measuring.

"Interested in guided fishing?" Derek asked.

"Fishing?" Evan replied. He looked at the brochure in his hand. "Yes. I have a month off work coming, and thought I'd go deep sea fishing."

"Very well, sir." Derek said, turning toward the basement door, and disappearing through it.

That night, Evan prepared his room carefully.

He wedged a chair beneath the door handle.

Shifted the dresser just enough to create resistance.

Not obvious.

Just enough.

Then he lay in bed, staring into darkness.

Tomorrow, he would contact John.

No matter what.

Whatever this place was —

It had gone far beyond coincidence.

CHAPTER 11

Evan barely slept.

Not because of fear — not exactly — but because his mind refused to disengage. Every time he drifted toward unconsciousness, another connection snapped into place, another implication surfaced, another realization clawed its way forward.

By morning, his exhaustion had sharpened into something hard and crystalline.

Resolve.

He rose early, before the lodge stirred fully to life, moving with quiet efficiency. Shower. Clothes. Shoes. Phone. Laptop. Notebook. All arranged neatly, deliberately, like tools laid out before a complicated repair.

Today, he was going to test the boundaries.

Every boundary.

He started with the guest phones.

They sat in their usual places — at the front desk, in the hallway alcoves, beside the lounge chairs. Simple, unobtrusive landlines. Nothing fancy. No visible branding. No obvious signs of restriction.

He lifted one and dialed.

Nothing.

No tone. No click. No static.

Just silence.

He hung up, tried another.

Still nothing.

He tried the phone in his room. Then the one near the dining hall. Then the wall-mounted unit by the rear exit.

All dead.

Not broken.

Disconnected.

His jaw tightened.

At the front desk, Jonah looked up as he set the receiver gently back in its cradle.

"The phones are still down?" Evan asked mildly.

His expression barely flickered. "Yes Mr. Mercer, but they should be fixed by tomorrow afternoon."

Evan nodded once. "Alright."

He didn't press.

Not yet.

He found Sam wiping down the bar, humming quietly to himself.

"Hey," Evan said, resting an elbow against the polished wood. "Quick question. Any idea when phone service is coming back up?"

Sam blinked once. "Phones?"

"Yeah, in the rooms."

"Oh." A half-second pause. "Shouldn't be long. We've had some signal interference lately. Weather-related, I think."

"Storms?"

"Atmospheric pressure shifts," Sam said easily. "They mess with satellite alignment."

Evan didn't let his face give anything away.

Evan studied him. "Satellite?"

Sam shrugged. "Whole lodge runs off a private satellite array. Keeps us off-grid. Management thing."

"Right," Evan said. "Of course." He kept a mental checklist of all the differing stories, thanked Sam, and moved on.

In the kitchen, Elena was prepping breakfast. The scent of coffee and warm bread filled the air.

"Morning," Evan said. "Is the internet acting weird for you too?"

She smiled without looking up. "It always does."

"Always?"

"Yeah. We don't have open internet. Just internal systems. Keeps things stable."

"Stable how?"

"Fewer variables," she said lightly. "Less risk."

"Risk of what?"

She finally glanced up at him, eyes soft, curious. "Why all the technical questions today?"

"Habit."

A beat.

"Well," she said, returning to her work, "Marlowe can explain it better than I can. She designed the infrastructure."

"Good to know," Evan said.

He left before the conversation could deepen.

By mid-morning, he was seated in the lounge with his laptop open.

No Wi-Fi networks.

Not even ghost signals.

He tried ethernet ports — hidden ones, tucked behind furniture and trim. Nothing. He scanned frequencies manually, cycling through known signal ranges.

There were signals.

Just not open ones.

He isolated them, traced their origin, mapped their behavior.

It took less than twenty minutes to confirm what he already suspected.

The lodge wasn't connected to the outside world at all.

Not directly.

Not even indirectly.

It operated on a closed satellite-based intranet loop — a sealed network that bounced internal communications between local terminals, remote storage hubs, and monitoring systems without ever touching public infrastructure.

Everything stayed inside.

Contained.

Like a terrarium.

Evan leaned back slowly, exhaling through his nose.

No outbound calls.

No external internet.

No emergency access.

No third-party routing.

Not even a weak leak.

A perfect seal.

This wasn't a retreat.

It was a cage.

By noon, the shift in atmosphere had become unmistakable.

Not overt.

Not hostile.

But present.

Jonah appeared more often, drifting casually into whatever room Evan occupied, striking up brief conversations before excusing himself.

Rosa checked on him twice during lunch.

Derek crossed his path three separate times in the span of twenty minutes — each encounter polite, each one unnecessary.

Even Marlowe emerged from her office once, offering a brief, warm smile as she passed.

"Everything comfortable today?" she asked.

"Yes," Evan replied.

"Good," she said, studying his face a second longer than needed. "Let us know if anything changes."

The message was gentle.

The meaning was not.

They were watching him more closely now.

Adjusting.

Compensating.

By mid-afternoon, Evan sat alone near the fire, notebook resting loosely on his knee.

There was no point pretending anymore.

No outside contact was possible.

Not by accident.

Not by failure.

By design.

Which meant there was only one way out.

Physical escape.

The realization settled slowly, heavily.

Not panic.

Not fear.

Calculation.

The lodge was surrounded by monitored forest. Wired trees. Buried cables. Hidden cameras. Sensor arrays.

But systems — no matter how elaborate — always had blind spots.

Human beings built them.

Human beings overlooked things.

And human beings grew complacent.

Evan closed his notebook and rose.

If the lodge was a closed system, then its boundaries had to exist somewhere.

And boundaries, by definition, could be crossed.

He spent the rest of the day moving deliberately, casually, mapping the rhythms of the place.

Staff rotations.

Meal schedules.

Maintenance routines.

Security overlaps.

He noted where presence clustered — and where it thinned.

The northern treeline remained the quietest zone.

Too steep for casual hiking.

Too dense for sightseeing.

Too inconvenient for guests.

And therefore — less monitored.

By early evening, his plan had begun to form.

Not fully.

Upstairs, he secured his room once more.

Chair.

Dresser.

Door.

Then he stood in the center of the darkened space, breathing slowly.

For the first time since arriving, the truth felt fully clear.

This place was not meant to be escaped.

Which meant that escape would not be simple.

He lay back on the bed, staring into darkness.

Tomorrow, he would test the perimeter.

Tomorrow, he would see just how real the forest truly was.

And whether it could be trusted more than the lodge itself.

Outside his window, the fog rolled in again — thicker than it had been all day.

Carefully.

Deliberately.

As if something were preparing.

CHAPTER 12

Evan really needed to call John.

The phone lines were still down, and his cell still had no service. He'd tried half a dozen times already, pacing the lodge's front porch, lifting the phone higher, angling it toward the sky, even standing on the tips of his boots like that might help. Nothing.

Derek had mentioned an electrified fence that ran along the perimeter of the property. Evan wondered if it might be acting like a Faraday cage, blocking whatever faint signal might reach this place. Maybe if he could get close enough to it—close enough to hold his phone beyond it—he could at least shoot John a text.

He remembered seeing what looked like a narrow path on the north side of the lodge. And hey, if it looked like a trail, it probably was one.

So he set off.

The forest wasn't dense, exactly. The trees were spaced far enough apart that sunlight still filtered down through the canopy, but thick underbrush crowded the ground, partially obscuring the path. And it was steep, too steep for a casual walk. Still, something—human or animal—had traveled this way often enough to wear a faint trail into the earth.

Evan followed it for what felt like hours. His watch told him it had only been a little over one, but time moved differently out here, stretched thin by the steady hush of the woods and the rhythmic crunch of leaves beneath his boots.

He knew he needed to turn back before dark. He also knew he needed to contact John. He needed to contact the outside world, he should've been in Longview days ago.

After another fifteen minutes, he spotted a small structure ahead.

At first, he thought it was an outhouse.

Curiosity nudged his steps toward it. As he drew closer, he saw it wasn't an outhouse at all, but some kind of outbuilding. Storage, maybe? A shed for maintenance tools? The lodge sprawled across acres of land, and it made sense they'd need equipment stashed throughout the property.

But the closer he got, the more that explanation unraveled.

The building was small. Too small. It might hold a rake or two, maybe a garden hose, but nothing that would justify its placement so far from the lodge. The walls were weathered, the wood warped and gray with age. The roof sagged slightly, as if it had long since surrendered the fight against gravity.

It looked abandoned.

Evan circled it, searching for a window. Finding none, he turned away, ready to continue his search for the fence.

He took three steps and froze.

There it was again.

That sound.

A low, steady hum, vibrating faintly in the air.

Electricity.

He'd heard it countless times before while working around pylons—the constant, living buzz of high-voltage lines. Sometimes it was so loud it drowned out traffic. This wasn't that powerful, but it was unmistakable.

And it was coming from this building.

Evan slowly turned back.

The hum grew louder as he approached the door. That made no sense. None at all. There was no power line nearby, no visible conduit, no reason for an old, half-rotted shed to be consuming electricity—let alone this much of it.

He reached for the doorknob and hesitated.

Before he even touched it, he knew it would be locked.

Sure enough, the knob didn't budge.

Up close, the door stood out in stark contrast to the rest of the structure. Where the walls and roof looked ancient, the door looked brand new. Heavy. Solid. The metal knob gleamed faintly in the dimming light, unscuffed, unmarred. Not just new, but high quality.

Someone had gone to effort here.

To anyone passing by, this might look like nothing more than a decaying shed. But anyone who stopped—anyone who really looked—would see it.

Someone wanted to keep people out.

Evan stepped back, unease creeping up his spine.

What could possibly be in there?

And why hide it like this?

For a moment, the temptation to pick the lock tugged at him. But the forest was already darkening, shadows stretching long across the ground. Whatever was inside, it wasn't worth getting lost out here after sunset.

He took one last look at the strange little building, then turned back toward the lodge.

Evan reached the edge of the clearing just as the last of the daylight began to thin. The sky beyond the trees was washed in muted blues and dying gold, the kind of quiet dusk that made even familiar places feel uncertain. The lodge windows glowed warmly ahead, a soft beacon against the encroaching dark.

As he stepped onto the gravel path, the front doors swung open.

Mrs. Calder stood in the doorway.

"Mr. Mercer!" she exclaimed, one hand flying to her chest as she hurried forward. "Oh, thank goodness. We were so worried when you didn't come back. We thought something had happened to you."

She reached him in two quick steps, her hands already fussing at his jacket, brushing dust from his sleeves, straightening his collar. Her palms were warm as she cupped his cheeks, her eyes scanning his face the way a mother might after her child had wandered too far.

"Are you hurt?" she asked softly. "Did you fall? You look exhausted."

"I just went for a walk, Mrs. Calder," Evan said, a little embarrassed by the attention. "Lost track of time, I guess."

Her frown lingered a moment longer before easing. "These woods aren't safe after dark. You must be careful."

Behind her, the soft murmur of voices filled the lobby. Jonah stood near the reception desk, a ledger tucked beneath his arm. He met Evan's eyes and let out an audible sigh.

"Mr. Mercer," he said gently, though there was a hint of reproach in his tone. "We told you not to wander too far. People disappear out here. Trails twist, fog rolls in, and suddenly you don't know which way is up anymore."

"I'm sorry," Evan said. "Really. I didn't mean to worry anyone."

Jonah gave a small, forgiving smile. "Just promise us you'll stay close to the lodge from now on."

"I promise."

The group slowly dispersed, returning to their quiet routines. Evan stood for a moment in the warm light of the lobby, feeling an unexpected flush of comfort. For a brief second, he felt like a wayward teenager who'd stayed out past curfew, greeted not with anger, but relief.

The scent of dinner drifted from the adjoining restaurant—roasted vegetables, warm bread, something savory simmering beneath it all. His stomach reminded him that he hadn't eaten since morning.

He followed the smell.

The dining room was softly lit, its windows dark mirrors now reflecting flickers of candlelight. Only a handful of guests were scattered among the tables, their voices low, subdued. Ian sat alone near the far wall, nursing a pint of beer and paging through something on his phone.

Evan hesitated, then gestured lightly.

"Mind if I sit?"

Ian looked up, then smiled. "Not at all. Please."

Evan pulled out the chair and settled across from him. "Evening."

"Evening," said Ian.

For nearly two hours, they talked over dinner. Using their mutual shorthand to discuss what Evan found that day.

By the time Evan finally headed to his room, the unease of the forest had faded into background static.

Morning came quietly.

Evan woke to muted light and the distant call of birds. For a moment, he lay still, letting the unfamiliar ceiling anchor him. The fog outside pressed faintly against the window, blurring the world into soft shapes.

He dressed and made his way downstairs, already thinking about breakfast and the conversation he'd left unfinished.

Ian's usual seat at the far table was empty.

That, in itself, meant nothing. He was recovering from a pretty nasty bug.

Still, Evan found his gaze lingering on the vacant chair longer than he intended.

The dining room was sparsely occupied. Rosa moved gently between tables, straightening linens, refilling cups. Sam stood behind the bar, polishing glassware, his attention seemingly split between his hands and the room beyond them. Near the service corridor, Miles wiped down a counter with careful, repetitive strokes.

Evan carried his coffee toward him.

"Hey," Evan said casually. "My friend — Ian. Did he head out already?"

Miles looked up.

For a fraction of a second, something flickered across his face. Not panic. Not fear.

Confusion.

Then uncertainty.

Then — just barely — something that looked like calculation.

It was gone almost immediately, smoothed beneath polite neutrality.

"I… I don't think so," Miles said. "I mean — I don't think there was a guest named Ian."

Evan let the words settle.

"What do you mean?" he asked gently.

Miles hesitated. His eyes shifted, briefly, toward the bar. Sam's back was to them, shoulders slightly hunched as he worked, humming softly under his breath.

"I handle room turnovers," Miles said. "Housekeeping logs. Key inventory. I would've seen his name."

"You're sure?"

Miles nodded, though the movement lacked conviction. "Positive."

A chill crept along Evan's spine.

Ian had been there since Evan got there.

They had compared schedules. Laughed about broken systems and outdated schematics.

They shared meals almost every day.

He played chess and pool with him.

"Maybe he checked out last night," Evan said.

Miles shook his head again cutting him off. "No one left overnight."

Evan stared at him.

"What about his room?"

"There... wasn't one," Miles said, and then stopped himself, lips pressing thin. "I mean — not that I'm aware of."

The words echoed unpleasantly.

Not that I'm aware of.

Evan nodded slowly, thanked him, and carried his coffee to the window.

Outside, the fog had thinned but not lifted. The trees loomed, their shapes distorted, their edges soft and uncertain. The forest looked less like a place and more like an idea.

He pulled out his phone.

No signal.

Of course.

Still, he scrolled through his contacts until he found the number Ian had typed in. *"When we both have some free time, we should go hunting or something."* That's what he said when he gave Evan his number. *'Ian Holloway – Rail Systems.'*

Evan stared at it.

Ian had been there.

He had proof.

And suddenly, the warmth of the lodge disappeared.

The memory of the outbuilding surfaced uninvited.

The hum of electricity.

The pristine lock.

The thought returned, no longer speculative:

What if he never left?

This time, it didn't settle like a stone.

It spread.

And Evan knew — with a certainty that left his stomach hollow — that he was going back into those woods.

Evan waited until midmorning before leaving the lodge.

Not because he was afraid of being seen — though he was — but because the place moved differently after breakfast. Guests drifted, staff dispersed, routines loosened. The tight choreography of morning softened into something more flexible, less attentive.

He took only what he needed.

His phone.

His lockpicks.

And a thin jacket against the persistent chill.

The forest swallowed him almost immediately.

The trail he'd followed the night before was easier to spot in daylight. Broken undergrowth, faint impressions in damp soil, a subtle logic to the way the land folded around itself. The fog hung low, threading through the trees like slow-moving smoke, thinning just enough to reveal the towering redwoods above.

The outbuilding emerged quietly from the haze.

Up close, it looked even more unassuming — a squat, weather-beaten structure barely larger than a garden shed. Peeling paint. Warped siding. A roof that sagged slightly under the weight of years. It looked like it belonged to another time entirely.

Nothing about it suggested power. Or technology. Or purpose.

Evan circled it slowly, listening.

Nothing.

He crouched at the door, sliding his fingers across the lock. It was high quality. Clean. Recently installed.

That alone made his pulse race upward.

He slipped his picks from his pocket and worked carefully, feeling for tension, reading the mechanism through touch alone. The lock yielded quickly — too quickly. Whoever had installed it valued strength, not subtlety.

The door opened with a faint whisper.

Inside, the space was barely larger than a school supply closet.

Metal shelving lined two walls, holding scattered maintenance items: a coil of hose, a half-empty box of filters, several buckets, a dented toolbox. A single fluorescent fixture hummed overhead, casting pale light across concrete flooring.

Nothing about it looked remarkable.

Evan stepped inside.

The door closed softly behind him.

He moved slowly, checking shelves, peering behind containers, tapping lightly on the walls. Everything felt solid. Real. Mundane.

After several minutes, he exhaled.

Nothing.

CHAPTER 13

A flicker of embarrassment touched him. He had let suspicion lead him into breaking and entering over… what? A bad feeling?

He reached for the light switch.

The room fell into darkness.

And in that instant, he saw it.

A pinprick of light.

No larger than the head of a nail, glowing faintly against the far wall near the floor.

Evan froze.

His breath slowed. His pulse steadied.

He turned carefully, angling his phone screen just enough to avoid washing out the glow. The light wasn't coming from the wall.

It was reflecting.

From a thin seam in the concrete.

He crouched, fingers tracing the faint outline of a rectangular panel set into the floor, its edges nearly invisible unless the light struck them just right.

A trap door.

There was no lock. No handle. Just a narrow metal groove.

Evan slipped his fingers inside and lifted.

The panel opened silently.

Cool air rushed upward, carrying with it the unmistakable hum of heavy electrical systems — layered, complex, alive.

A ladder descended into darkness.

Evan hesitated only a moment before stepping onto the rungs.

The air changed as he climbed down — cooler, drier, humming with hidden energy. The ladder ended in a narrow corridor, barely wide enough for his shoulders, the concrete walls pressing close on either side.

The deeper he went, the louder the hum became.

Not chaotic.

Organized.

Intentional.

The hallway bent sharply, then descended again. Tight turns. Low ceilings. The architecture forced him forward, deeper, further from the surface, until the air felt thick with machinery and buried purpose.

Finally, the corridor opened.

Evan stepped onto an elevated metal platform.

Below him stretched a vast underground chamber.

Control racks lined the walls in precise rows. Monitors flickered with live camera feeds. Pressure gauges pulsed steadily. Signal readouts scrolled data in endless streams. Thick cable bundles vanished into conduit channels that disappeared into the surrounding earth.

He stood motionless.

Fog pressure systems.

Radio transmitters.

Signal jammers.

Directional antenna controls.

Hydraulic flow indicators.

GPS interference mapping.

Tree lift actuators.

It was all here.

Not scattered.

Not improvised.

Engineered.

A system.

Evan moved slowly along the platform, phone in hand, capturing image after image. Each station told part of the story, each readout reinforcing what his instincts had been assembling piece by piece.

The fog hadn't been natural.

The radio broadcasts hadn't been coincidence.

The GPS failures hadn't been atmospheric.

The fallen tree hadn't been chance.

It wasn't the forest that hunted travelers.

It was people.

People wearing the forest's face.

He thought of the power meter. The excuse about the electrified fence. The hum beneath the lodge. The comforting smiles. The gentle reassurances.

Everything aligned.

The lodge wasn't shelter.

It was the center of a trap.

A soft sound echoed behind him.

Not machinery.

Footsteps.

Evan turned.

And the system, finally aware of him, began to close.

Evan froze. The footsteps — slow, purposeful — echoed off the concrete walls. He pressed himself into the shadow beneath the platform, holding his breath. Every nerve in his body screamed to move, but he knew even a slight shift could give him away.

A voice cut through the hum of electricity. Low. Controlled. Male.

"I don't care who's nephew he is, the kid is a liability."

Evan's stomach sank. The voice belonged to Derek Hollen. But there was no second voice in the room. Derek was on the phone, and the way he held it, tapping occasionally against his shoulder, meant he wasn't expecting company.

Evan strained to listen, every word driving a nail into his chest.

"He as good as told Mercer that Holloway checked out. Holloway isn't supposed to have existed! If it were up to me, the kid would've already had a blanket party by now."

Evan's breath stopped. *Blanket Party?* What'd that mean?

"If Elena could get the dosing right, Mercer wouldn't even remember Holloway. He'd think this was all a dream."

Silence again while the person on the other end of the conversation responded.

"Whatever, Caleb. I'm on my way to fell the tree now. You sure this woman has money?"

Caleb. Why did that name sound familiar?

Derek continued. "Did you call Jonah already to set the jammers? I don't want to get back to the I—" He broke off, as if realizing something mid-sentence. "...the lodge and... Hey, they didn't do Mercer yet, did they? I didn't get a page for cleanup."

There was a pause as Caleb's voice answered, faint and distorted over the line.

"I don't see him on any of the monitors."

Evan pressed himself flatter, heart hammering. *"Dosing"*? *"Do Mercer?"* What the fuck was going on here? Derek was stepping closer, his boots scraping lightly against the metal floor. Evan's mind raced. *If he turns this way, he'll see me.*

Derek muttered into the phone, low enough Evan almost couldn't hear:

"Let Sam know that I can't see him on the monitors. I'm going to scrub the footage to see if I can find where he went. Guy likes to wander off."

Evan waited, motionless, counting every heartbeat. The hum of machinery seemed louder now, oppressive. The cables overhead, the panels, the faint blinking lights — all of it pulsed in rhythm with his own panicked pulse.

And then Derek's shadow moved across the platform. He hadn't seen Evan — yet.

Evan didn't hesitate. He sprinted, moving as quietly as he could toward the ladder. Derek's voice barked into the phone behind him.

"Caleb, I swear — if Mercer got out, I'll—"

Evan ducked, rolling behind a console, the edge scraping his jacket. His phone slipped from his pocket. A quiet *click* echoed. Derek froze, just for a heartbeat, then continued talking, unaware.

Evan grabbed the phone, crouched, and darted toward a shadow, toward a narrow maintenance corridor he had noticed before.

That's when it hit him — the realization, sudden and sharp: Caleb. *He'd seen him at the gas station. The smile. The charm. That's how they'd known when to trap him.*

Evan's stomach roiled. The attendant was part of this. Had always been part of it.

A turn in the hallway brought him face-to-face with Derek. Derek's eyes narrowed, and he made a move toward Evan.

Evan didn't think. He shoved a small metal rolling shelf from along the wall into Derek's chest, enough to stagger him. Derek lunged — the scrape of boots and the thud of impact echoing like thunder.

Evan bolted past him, heart screaming, adrenaline coiling like steel. The corridor narrowed, forcing him to duck beneath exposed pipes. The hum of electricity seemed to pulse in time with his own sprinting heart.

Above, he could hear Derek curse, then the phone dropping with a clatter. A moment later, boots pounding behind him — Derek. And faint, hurried footsteps echoing behind those, lighter, quicker — Was it Caleb?

Evan's mind flashed — numbers, monitors, cameras, the ladder, the trap door. Everything was designed to shepherd him, guide him. To corral him. To punish him.

And yet... he could use it against them.

He veered into a maintenance alcove, ducked behind stacked crates, and snapped a quick picture with his phone — just enough to capture the cable banks and monitors, the control panels. Evidence. If he survived.

Then he ran.

Every turn became a strategy. Every shadow a potential path. Every sound a misdirection to exploit. The system was vast, precise — but it didn't know he understood it now.

And with each step, the forest outside, somehow, felt aware. Protective. Not attacking. Guiding.

Evan's pulse thundered. He had to escape — but one thought stayed with him, sharpening with terror and clarity:

Ian Holloway isn't suppose to have existed. But he did.

Another set of footsteps joined the pursuit.

Lighter. Faster.

A woman's voice echoed faintly through the tunnels — sharp, alert. "Derek?"

"Elena! Down here!" Derek shouted behind him.

Evan's heart sank. There were more of them. Was everyone in on it?

The corridors twisted unpredictably, branching and reconnecting, some sloping upward, others plunging deeper into the earth. Pipes lined the ceilings, vibrating faintly with pressure. Cable bundles hung like thick vines, forcing Evan to duck and weave.

He took turns blindly.

Left. Right. Down. Then up again.

Every corridor looked the same.

Every corner felt like a trap.

Somewhere behind him, more voices called out. Commands. Warnings. Directional cues. Their coordination was tight, practiced.

This wasn't a scramble.

It was a hunt.

Evan's lungs burned as he sprinted, boots slapping against concrete. He slid around a corner and nearly collided with a metal storage rack. Bottles clinked as he shoved past it, the sound echoing wildly through the narrow space.

He ran harder.

A low hum rose suddenly in pitch. Lights flickered. For a moment, the tunnels pulsed in dim red before returning to their normal sterile glow.

Evan didn't slow.

Behind him, someone cursed.

He darted into another corridor, only to find it narrowing until the walls nearly brushed his shoulders. His breath sounded impossibly loud in the confined space.

Footsteps thundered behind him.

Just when it felt like they were about to catch him, a junction appeared ahead — one that hadn't been there seconds earlier.

A short service ladder climbed toward a circular hatch.

Evan didn't question it.

He took the rungs two at a time, shoving the hatch upward with a grunt and spilling into open air.

Fog swallowed him instantly.

The forest loomed, dense and shifting, branches arching overhead like vaulted ceilings. The chill air shocked his lungs as he staggered forward, boots sinking into damp soil.

Shouts echoed behind him.

Flashlights cut through the fog like knives.

Branches cracked.

Evan ran.

The woods twisted unpredictably, shadows sliding and reforming between the trees. Every time his pursuers sounded close — every time he felt hot breath at his back — something intervened.

A fallen limb sent one of them sprawling.

Underbrush that scratched his face, turned into walls of briars behind him.

Fog thinned in areas ahead of him. He ran into the thin areas, only to have it thicken behind him an instant later.

A sudden gust scattered leaves into his pursuer's faces, blinding them.

Paths appeared where moments before there had been only tangled undergrowth.

Evan's legs screamed. His chest burned. His vision narrowed to the narrow strip of ground ahead of him.

And then — pavement.

Highway 101 burst from the fog like a revelation.

Evan stumbled onto the shoulder, and saw a man across the highway.

"They're everywhere! How many were there?" Evan thought to himself.

He turned around and couldn't even see the huge redwood trunks anymore the fog was so thick. He also couldn't hear his pursuers anymore.

Turning to face the man across from him, he prepared for a fight. But there was no man.

Evan froze. A trick of the fog and the underbrush. It had to be. Was there ever a man across the road?

As Evan stood there trying to determine his next move, a light breeze blew towards him.

It was nice, calming, salty. The sea. He must be facing west. He turned to look behind him again, and the dense fog was gone. The fog itself wasn't gone, but it looked... natural. Real.

Making up his mind, he turned to his left, and started walking south, passing mile marker 77.

After some time, the adrenaline that enabled him to run to freedom, finally wore off. Evan collapsed to his knees, then lost consciousness.

Hands grabbed his shoulders roughly.

"Sir! Sir can you hear me?" A voice shouted.

Evan couldn't answer.

He could feel the sun warming the right side of his face, and when he opened his eyes a millimeter, he saw flashing lights. Emergency lights?

"Sir! Sir can you open your eyes for me?" The voice said again. "Roll medical to my location." It said quieter, but with the same urgency.

Evan closed his eyes again. "Wh — " Evan started to say.

Then he remembered. His eyes flew open, he jumped to his feet, fists raised, ready to fight.

"Hold on now sir!" A man said taking a non-aggressive stance, a man with a badge.

Evan kept still, but didn't lower his guard just yet. He spun around, looking for the Native American man again.

"What's your name?" The deputy asked.

"My – Evan. My name is Evan. Mercer." He lowered his arms a fraction.

"Okay Mr. Mercer," The deputy replied, indicating to Evan that he could relax. "What happened? Do you need medical attention?"

"N – no, ye – maybe, I don't know."

"Cancel medical." The deputy said into his shoulder radio. "Have them meet us at the station."

Evan lowered his hands and scanned his surroundings. The fog was still a light mist, but now the sun was shining through the redwoods. It was almost peaceful.

"Mr. Mercer, come with me. We'll get you some help, okay?" The deputy stepped closer to Evan and placed one hand on his shoulder to guide him to the passenger side of the cruiser.

"Yeah," Said Evan still looking around. "yeah, help."

As he sat in the cruiser next to the deputy, he started to feel comfortable. More comfortable than he had in the last 24 hours. And as the deputy drove, Evan rested his head against the passenger window, watching the trees fly past. For a moment, he thought he saw the Native American man again. Evan saw him just long enough for the man to nod, then he was gone.

CHAPTER 14

Once the deputy got Evan to the station, there was an ambulance already waiting.

They checked Evan over and determined that he didn't need to go to the hospital.

The sheriff let him use the phone to call John. He had been out of contact with him for seven days. Evan remembered thinking that couldn't be true, but time at the lodge seemed to move differently.

After the ambulance left, the sheriff gave Evan a glass of water and gestured toward the metal bench against the wall. "Take a seat."

Evan lowered himself slowly, muscles still trembling from exertion. His clothes were streaked with mud and pine needles. His hands shook as he brought the glass to his lips, spilling more than he drank.

Across the room, two deputies murmured quietly. One typed at a computer terminal. The other kept glancing up at Evan, brows furrowed.

"Let's go through this again," the sheriff finally said, pulling a chair over. "From the top."

Evan dragged a hand down his face.

"I was staying at a lodge," he said. "Off Highway 101. Remote. Deep woods. Staff of six. Maybe more."

The sheriff nodded slowly.

"Name of the lodge?"

"I—I don't know the official name. They just called it the lodge."

Another look passed between them.

"And you're saying this lodge is where, exactly?"

Evan pointed vaguely northeast. "A few miles past the old turnout. There's a narrow paved road, barely marked."

The deputy typed something, then turned the monitor slightly.

A satellite map filled the screen.

"That area is all protected forest," he said. "No buildings. No registered businesses. No private roads."

Evan leaned forward. "That's not possible. I was there. There were guests. Cabins. Power lines. Staff housing. Tunnels under the property—"

"Tunnels," the younger deputy repeated.

Evan stopped.

The older sheriff held up a hand. "Slow down. You mentioned a man named Derek."

"Yes." Evan nodded eagerly. "Derek Hollen. Or—something. Tall. Dark hair. Scar on his jaw. Early forties, maybe."

Both deputies shook their heads.

"No Hollens in our system." the older one said.

"He worked there," Evan insisted. "He was part of it. He—" Evan swallowed. "He was the maintenance guy."

"Anybody else?" Asked the sheriff. "Your rental car was two miles back with two blown tires. All your luggage was in it still. You were disoriented, dehydrated, barefoot and clearly injured."

"I wasn't barefoot," Evan said.

The deputy pointed at his feet.

Evan looked down.

His socks were shredded. His shoes were gone.

His stomach dropped.

Silence settled over the room, thick and uncomfortable.

"Tell us everyone you remember," the older deputy said quietly. "All the names."

Evan squeezed his eyes shut for a second, forcing his thoughts to line up.

"Marlowe Trent," he said. "She ran the place. Jonah... Pike —he was the receptionist." Evan hesitated, then continued. "Who else... let me think..."

The deputies exchanged a brief glance.

"There was Elena," Evan added. "The cook… I think she was drugging us. Sam the bartender. Rosa – er… Mrs. Calder, hospitality and this kid, uh… Miles… something. Miles… Greene… Graham… Grant… he was the busboy."

As the younger deputy typed steadily, the sheriff looked momentarily pale. Evan almost didn't catch it.

"Nothing," murmured the younger deputy.

Evan's throat tightened. "And Derek Hollen." He finished lamely.

The room remained quiet.

"That's quite a group." the older deputy said gently.

Evan shook his head. "You don't understand. They were hiding *people. Killing* them!"

The older deputy's brow creased. "Easy son."

"There was another guest," Evan said. "Ian Holloway. We talked for days. Ate together, played pool, chess."

Both deputies looked up. The room stayed silent.

"I talked to him, every day…" Evan insisted. "He existed."

The younger deputy turned his monitor toward Evan.

"No Ian Holloway," the deputy said. "No birth certificate. No phone records. No financial activity. No travel. Nothing."

"Then they erased him." Evan whispered.

The older deputy studied him carefully now.

"And you believe this Marlowe Trent did that."

"Yes." Evan nodded. "She designed it. She had to have!" Evan said, nearly rising from his seat.

Neither deputy nor the sheriff spoke.

"Ian wasn't supposed to have existed," Evan said. "Derek said it himself. Just before he found me in the control room."

The older deputy folded his hands slowly. "Mr. Mercer... do you hear how this sounds?"

Evan closed his eyes.

"Yes."

"And your phone?" the younger deputy asked. "You mentioned pictures."

Evan reached into his pocket.

Nothing.

Cold panic surged through him. He searched every pocket, every fold of fabric. His hands brushed broken plastic and sharp edges.

He pulled out what remained of his phone.

The screen was shattered beyond recognition. The casing bent inward. The camera lens cracked clean through, a spiderweb of fractures reflecting the harsh fluorescent light.

"I *had* pictures," Evan said weakly. "I took pictures. Of the tunnels. Of the equipment. Of—"

The deputy accepted the ruined phone, turning it gently in his hands, examining the damage.

"Looks like it took a pretty hard hit."

Evan stared at the mangled device as it was handed back. "Yeah," he mumbled. "I must have fallen." He finished weakly.

The words sounded thin, even to him.

They gave him some time to get cleaned up.

A locker room tucked behind the holding area. A clean towel. Clean clothes. A pair of boots that didn't quite fit but felt like luxury after torn socks and bare pavement. The hot water stung his cuts and bruises, but he welcomed it. Let it wash away the dirt. The blood. The forest.

When he stepped back into the main area, dressed and steadier, one of the deputies nodded toward the front windows.

"Your car's ready."

Outside, his rental sat in the bright afternoon sun, two brand-new tires replacing the shredded ones. A mobile mechanic was just packing up his tools.

"Lucky timing," the deputy said. "He was already in the area."

They walked him through directions, tracing a finger along a printed map. How to get back to I-5. Which turns to avoid. Where the road narrowed. Where service should return, and the nearest place he could get a new phone.

"Drive safe," the older deputy said, meeting Evan's eyes. "And if you remember anything else—anything at all—call."

Evan nodded.

As he made his way out the front door of the sheriff's station, the sheriff held out his hand and Evan took it.

"Drive safe Mr. Mercer. Don't take any side roads, stick to the route the deputies showed you."

"Absolutely Sheriff – " Evan's eyes raked the man's chest. "Grant. I won't take anymore detours."

He walked to his rental car and slid into the driver's seat, turning the key.

The engine came to life. The radio crackled, then settled into a local rock station. A song by *Warrant* drifted through the speakers.

'Uncle Tom's Cabin' maybe.

He turned the volume down so it became little more than background noise.

As he pulled onto the road, doubt crept in.

Was it real?

The fog. The tunnels. The machines. The voices. The chase.

What if he *had* been in an accident? What if he'd hit his head, wandered into the woods, and got lost for seven days? His phone was destroyed. His memory felt scrambled. His body ached in ways that suggested falls he couldn't recall.

What if none of it had happened?

The thought lingered as the miles slipped by.

Then—

Ding.

The gas light blinked on.

Evan exhaled sharply.

He slowed as the familiar shape of a gas station came into view. He had to have driven past it on his way north last time, and as he did, memory surged forward unbidden. The single pump. The flickering lights. The weathered canopy.

He pulled in.

An older man stepped out, wiping his hands on a rag. He had a lined face and a faint country accent that softened his voice.

"What can I get ya?"

"Fill. Regular." Evan replied in a flat voice.

The man nodded and began fueling.

"Hey," Evan started, hesitating. "You got a kid named Caleb working here?"

The old man shook his head. "Naw. Friend of yours?"

"No." Evan said. "No, I must have the wrong station."

The man shrugged easily and returned to the pump.

Evan stared straight ahead, jaw clenched.

When the tank was full, he paid, thanked him, and drove off.

I-5 felt like sanctuary.

Evan merged northbound and let himself breathe for the first time since the forest. Cars filled every lane. The press of humanity, once suffocating, now felt like protection.

He had always hated freeways.

Now, they made him feel safe.

Hours passed. His body demanded a restroom, and he needed to stretch his legs. He pulled into a sprawling truck stop beside a strip mall, filled his tank, emptied his bladder, bought a soda that tasted like pure sugar and chemicals. Familiar.

That was when he saw the phone store.

Bright lights. Clean glass. Corporate normalcy.

He drove over to it, and parked.

Inside, he placed the broken remains of his phone gently on the counter. The salesperson stared at it in open horror.

"What happened?"

"Forgot it on the roof of the car." Evan said, jerking his thumb over his shoulder, not making eye contact. He knew his face and hands told a different story.

The salesperson worked carefully, extracting the SIM card. He examined it for a long moment.

"Still intact," the salesperson murmured, impressed. "You're lucky."

A few minutes later, Evan stepped back into the early evening, powered on his new phone, and leaned against his car.

He still hadn't called his boss.

Scrolling through his contacts, his thumb paused on its way to the "J"s.

There, at the beginning of the "I"s —

Ian Holloway.

Evan's breath caught.

His blood turned to ice.

The name sat there, simple and undeniable.

Not imagined.

Not erased.

Not gone.

Ian had been real.

It all had been real.

EPILOGUE

One year later.

The highway stretched ahead in a long, pale ribbon, cutting through rolling farmland and low hills softened by early morning fog. The sky was wide and colorless, dawn still deciding what it wanted to be.

Evan drove with both hands on the wheel.

Not rigid. Not tense.

Just… present.

The newspaper lay folded on the passenger seat, creased from being opened and closed too many times. The headline was visible even from his peripheral vision.

FINAL SENTENCINGS DELIVER CLOSURE IN LODGE CASE

He didn't need to read it again.

He already knew every word.

The article detailed the end of the trials — the last of them, at least. The convictions. The plea deals. The sentencing. The federal asset seizures. The destruction of the lodge itself, dismantled down to its bones, the surrounding land excavated, the buried infrastructure ripped free from the earth.

Satellite   arrays   confiscated.
Underground   corridors   collapsed.
Wiring stripped from the forest like veins torn from flesh.

The place had been erased.

Not abandoned.

Not shuttered.

Erased.

The official investigations had spanned three states and two federal agencies, uncovering a system far larger than anyone had initially imagined. Dozens of shell companies. Offshore accounts. Logistics pipelines built to move people, vehicles, and data without ever brushing against public networks.

The lodge had not been an isolated anomaly.

It had been a node.

A hub.

And when it fell, the network unraveled.

Slowly at first.

Then all at once.

The paper didn't mention Evan by name.

Just *a guest whose testimony proved pivotal.*

That suited him fine.

The deceased had never been recovered.

Despite months of excavation, sonar sweeps, forest searches, and ground-penetrating radar, no bodies were found. No graves. No remains. Nothing definitive.

Only the vehicles.

Stripped to frames. VIN numbers filed down. Engines parted out. Components sold through black-market distribution channels that had been operating for years under legitimate business fronts.

Evidence of profit.

Nothing else.

The living victims were another story.

Once Miles Grant finally cracked — truly cracked — the dam burst.

It took nearly three months of pressure, isolation, and confrontation before he broke completely. But when he did, he gave them everything.

Routes.

Codes.

Drop locations.

Transfer schedules.

False permits.

Encrypted backups.

Hidden facilities.

And names.

So many names.

The victims that were recovered came from multiple states.

Families were reunited.

Others were simply informed.

The human cost spanned thousands of pages of testimony and victim impact statements.

Miles received a reduced sentence.

Twenty years.

Eligible for parole in twelve.

The court called it *cooperation-based leniency.*

The media called it *unforgivable mercy.*

Miles called it *insufficient.*

His uncle, Sheriff Grant, was not afforded the same grace.

The evidence against him had been overwhelming.

Missing persons cases redirected. Search warrants delayed. Patrol routes altered. Evidence misfiled. Witness statements buried. Tips discarded. Jurisdictional confusion deliberately manufactured.

All of it signed. All of it documented.

All of it treasonous to the oath he'd sworn.

He received life without parole.

The courtroom had been silent when the sentence was read.

The radio murmured softly from the dashboard.

A true-crime podcast. One of dozens that had sprung up almost overnight.

"...a textbook example of systemic exploitation hidden behind the illusion of safety and comfort," the host was saying. "What's most disturbing is how easily it operated for so long. This wasn't just criminal ingenuity — this was institutional failure."

Evan reached over and turned it off.

Silence flooded the car.

A moment later, he tapped the screen again, pulling up a saved playlist.

Music filled the cabin — steady, instrumental, wordless.

Better.

The freeway unrolled ahead of him, taking him east.

He hadn't driven like this in years.

Not really.

Not without tension.

Not without calculating exits, scanning mirrors, mapping contingencies.

The freeway accident still lived in his bones.

But the road ahead now felt… negotiable.

Not safe.

Not comforting.

Just passable.

He passed a weathered green sign:

NEXT SERVICES — 42 MILES

Plenty of time.

Plenty of road.

His testimony was behind him now.

Depositions. Cross-examinations. Federal hearings. Grand juries. Closed-door briefings with agencies that never introduced themselves properly.

He had answered every question.

Given every detail.

Turned over every observation.

And when it was done, they had let him go.

Not with gratitude.

With distance.

That was fine too.

Evan drove.

The land shifted gradually, flattening, fields looming on both sides of him.

At a rest stop, he pulled over briefly, standing beside the car and letting the sun warm his shoulders as he moved his legs to return circulation. Trucks idled nearby. Coffee steamed from open cups. Somewhere, a dog barked.

Life, happening.

Ordinary.

He stood there for a long moment, then returned to the driver's seat and continued on.

The road unwound beneath him.

And with it, the weight of a year slowly loosened its grip.

Not gone.

But no longer crushing.

He drove toward the next assignment.

Another isolated job site.

Another remote installation.

Another system waiting to be built.

The world was still full of closed spaces.

Still full of hidden corners.

Still full of structures designed to contain and conceal.

But now, he knew how to see them.

And how to leave.

The highway stretched ahead, vanishing into distant light.

Evan followed it.

Author's Note: On the Watchers of the Grove

The supernatural elements in *Mile Post 77* are inspired by the oral traditions of Indigenous tribes native to Northern California and Southern Oregon, particularly the Yurok, Karuk, Hupa, and Tolowa peoples.

Many tribes in this region told stories of small forest beings, often referred to today as Stick Indians or The Little People — entities believed to inhabit remote forests, capable of misleading travelers, mimicking voices, and protecting sacred lands.

These stories were traditionally passed down orally and varied by region, family, and era. Out of respect, this novel does not attempt to replicate any single tradition directly, but instead weaves elements of multiple legends into a fictional mythos.

Readers interested in learning more may explore ethnographic collections, tribal oral histories, and regional folklore archives for deeper understanding.

Continue Evan's story in _The Last Dock_

Coming soon.